The Marvellous Land of Snergs

E. A. Wyke-Smith

Nebula

Cover images from pixabay.com

Organized and designed by Lu Evans

https://www.facebook.com/nebula.literature

Printed in the United States of America, 2018

About the author

E. A. Wyke-Smith (1871 – 1935) was an English adventurer, mining engineer and writer.

Wyke-Smith began writing fantasy tales for his children as an apparent antidote to the experience of World War I. He wrote his first book, Bill of the Bustingforths, at his children's request. He went on to write several others, both for children and adults.

J. R. R. Tolkien, is known to have read, The Marvellous Land of Snergs to his children. The similarities between the races of snergs and hobbits have led to speculation that the Snergs were a major inspiration for Tolkien's Hobbits. They are similar in their physical descriptions, their love of communal feasting, and their names, particularly Gorbo and Bilbo. In both books there are also journeys through dangerous forests and underground caverns.

Works

Bill of the Bustingforths (1921)
The Last of the Baron (1921)
Some Pirates and Marmaduke (1921)
Captain Quality (1922)
The Second Chance (1923)
Because of Josephine (1924)
Fortune My Foe (1925)
The Marvellous Land of Snergs (1927)

The Marvellous Land of Snergs

PART I

A PLACE APART

If any seafaring person, such as a yachtsman, were to sail round the corner of Watkyns Bay in the morning, he would find large numbers of children playing in the water, and would be either pleased or depressed at the sight according to the way his nature was originally formed. Certainly he would wonder how they came to be there, in such a lonely place and so very much at home, the little ones splashing about in the shallow parts and chasing each other over the sand, and the bigger ones swimming out to rafts and diving from them, and all shouting and squeaking. But this is a case of supposing, for no yacht or any other vessel will ever round the corner of the bay and no sail will ever be seen on the skyline, the reason being that it is the land of the S.R.S.C. and therefore a place set apart. If a yachtsman were ever tempted to sail in that direction he would be met by baffling winds from the nor'-east, alternating with baffling winds from the sou'-west, and this, combined with the prevalence of waterspouts, would make him repent of his purpose, and he could consider himself lucky if he got out of those waters lashed to what was left of the mast.

There is one exception to the rule that no outsider can sail near there, and that is the case of Vanderdecken and his men, who put in and camped some two and a half miles north of the bay. Owing to his rash oath that he would beat round the Cape of Good Hope if he beat round it till Doomsday he found himself doing so, and though this was rough luck on his crew, who had not made any rash oaths, naturally they had to beat round with him. It is supposed that the curse wore thin after a few hundred years; at any rate they managed to slip into the waters of the S.R.S.C. during the vernal equinox, and there they are now, camped in little huts, with the ship anchored in the mouth of a river and in a shocking state of barnacles.

MISS WATKYNS

The bay is named after Miss Watkyns, who is not only the Principal but the originator of the S.R.S.C., or Society for the Removal of Superfluous Children. Like a good many ladies who have no children of their own she was greatly interested in them, and being a little interfering in her ways she became in time a noted figure in police courts and was often laughed at by the public. This brought her in contact with other ladies similarly disposed and finally the Society was formed, its object being the removal of children who are obviously not wanted by their parents, or parent as the case may be. The greatest care is taken to void mistakes, but once a child is removed it is never returned, and it soon forgets what happened when it was with its parents (or parent) for the air of the place is splendid for forgetting. There are cases where, after some years with the Society (or what would be some years if time counted there in the ordinary way), a child is delivered over to some person who ardently desires one; but the selection of such a person needs even greater care to avoid mistakes.

Miss Watkyns is a lady of intelligence far above the ordinary, and in addition to being a great organizer she has no mean knowledge of the sciences. These qualities enabled her not only to discover the existence of the Land of the Snergs (in itself a marvellous piece of brain work) but also how to get there without a nasty spill. I do not propose to go into details of how she managed this (as it would take a book twice as long as this one) but will merely state that she admitted into the Society twenty-two carefully selected ladies (each of whom had four or five children ready to be removed from their homes without notice) and made the most careful preparations for transferring them all to the new land.

It was arranged that each lady should come with one well wrapped up superfluous child, as this would be all that they could carry at one time and the rest could be fetched later. They were to bring also for each one a bundle containing blankets, woollies, and two combination suits of wear-resisting fabric, and to use their discretion with regard to small extras, such as wash rags, fine tooth combs and the like. All went excellently. They met on Hampstead Heath one blowy October night at 11.30, and by 12.15 Miss Watkyns had inspected and passed all bundles and seen that all hands had taken a cup of hot milk or cocoa. Then she gave the word and away they all went on a high wind.

From this slight beginning grew the organization of the S.R.S.C. as it is to-day, with 478 superfluous children under its care and more coming. As this is purely a narrative of the extraordinary adventures that befell two of the children owing to their foolish disregard of the laws so wisely made for their benefit (a narrative which should not be without improving effect on the minds of my younger readers), I will not give more than a brief account of the ways and means by which the Society attains its object.

WAYS AND MEANS

The children are divided into two classes, according to size and age. The little ones wear one-piece garments known as the "slip-on," which have the advantage that they can be slipped off for bathing with one wriggle. The older ones wear two-piece garments; the boys having shorts and shirts and the girls skirts and blouses. Woolly coats are worn in the cold weather, which lasts only for a few seasonal weeks at Christmas time. For most of the year they do not wear shoes, but what are called slinkers.

The houses are on the higher ground just behind Watkyns Bay, and are all of one story. They are made of a criss-cross framework of timbers, with walls of clay mixed with little mashed-up shells in between the timbers, very strong and neat in appearance. Inside, the walls are plastered and painted light pink or blue. Behind the houses there is a wide stretch of turf, on which are swings and arrangements for healthful games such as net-ball and bumble-puppy. Not far away the forest begins with few trees at first and mostly bushes, where they play at pretence Indians and Robin Hood and so forth; but the trees soon grow thicker and thicker until it is quite shady even at midday in some parts. A pleasant place, with soft lawns here and there and a variety of ferns, but it is not wise to let the children roam about there too much for it is quite easy to get lost. Beyond the forest, a long day's march away, is the town of the Snergs, who built the houses for the Society as well as doing other useful things of which I will give an account later.

Each house has a protecting fence twelve feet from the walls to keep away the cinnamon bears, who live in the forest and who form friendships with the children when on their walks. This is all very well in its way, but the bears had the habit of trying to get into the houses at night, and, when they found the doors shut, of lying down outside and rubbing against the walls at intervals, which kept the children awake and made them giggle and whisper in a silly way, so the fence was put up. The bears are of fair size, with softish fur smelling slightly of cinnamon, hence the name. They must not be confused with the large grizzly bears which, rumour has it, live beyond the deep river on the other side of the Snerg country, as also tigers, unicorns, a dragon or two, and other creatures full of original sin.

With the exception of the very little ones each child has to attend to its own bed, and on Saturdays to refill the mattresses with little buds like hops, which have a pleasant aromatic smell and induce sleep. The old hops are thrown out on the beach at high tide. Saturday is the clean-up time. Lockers are tidied, pinafores are ironed, and puppies and other animals that need it are washed with soap; altogether there is a good deal of what the Gentlemen of the Life Guards call spit and polish, so as to be ready for Sunday. The smallest children have beds with rockers, Miss Watkyns having little patience with newfangled ideas about not rocking children.

A good deal of worry and argument has been caused by the amount of animal life in and round about the houses. There is a craze for pets, and Miss Watkyns' attempt to limit at the rate of one pet animal to each three children resulted in quarrels and sulking in corners, and finally it came to the rule of one child one animal. Puppies, kittens and small rabbits are the most popular; badgers are discouraged. At one time the elder children got excited over a recitation from the poets concerning a girl who owned a lamb which followed her about everywhere, even to school, where it made the other scholars laugh, and after that it was nothing but lambs. At length Miss Watkyns decided that only those who showed perfect behaviour for a month could have one, and that limited the number right enough. At the end of the month only two smug little girls had qualified for lambs, and by that time the rage for mongeese had come up.

Another source of trouble over animals is the food question. The ladies as a rule are rather sentimental in their ideas and it needed all the firmness and common sense of Miss Watkyns to prevent a wave of sloppiness passing over the Society and damaging the children's character and insides. Some even went to the length of proposing that the food should consist entirely of bread, butter, milk, and green stuff; and the experiment was actually tried for a time, with the result that the children broke out in pimples. Then fish diet was added, it being supposed that fish feel no pain when they are caught, only a little regret, but this was also a failure; the little ones' systems still cried out for meat and gravy in moderation. Finally, Miss Watkyns put her foot down firmly and arranged that a supply of sheep and hares, etc., be delivered at regular intervals by the Snergs, who are not at all sentimental about killing animals; in fact they rather like it, being great hunters.

THE SNERGS

The Snergs are a race of people only slightly taller than the average table but broad in the shoulders and of great strength. Probably they are some offshoot of the pixies who once inhabited the hills and forests of England, and who finally disappeared about the reign of Henry VIII. Their language is not very difficult and the children especially learn to speak it in a few weeks, which helps to strengthen my theory of their origin. The ladies, however, never learn to speak the language with fluency, and the little slang expressions are quite beyond them; but owing to the untiring energy of Miss Watkyns, that brainy woman, they now have a little Snerg grammar, with a vocabulary and some easy exercises.

The Snergs took a great interest in the Society's development and offered their services at an early date. It soon came to pass that they did all the heavy work, such as building (at which they are expert), gardening, painting and decorating, and the more troublesome part of the housework, such as swabbing floors. They come in batches and spend some weeks at work; then they say they are homesick, which means they have got tired of it, and they go home as soon as another batch can take their place. In return for these services they receive instruction in up-to-date methods from Miss Watkyns' Encyclopaedia, little presents from London or some other large town when one of the ladies has gone there on business, and those little general advantages, difficult to specify in words, which come from intercourse with refined females.

If the children go to the woods to collect berries or mushrooms or whatever else happens to be in season, or to play at outlaws or a little scalping party, a

Snerg or two goes with them to shoo away obtrusive bears. When they are bathing a Snerg or two sits on a rock ready to dive in and pick out any child that has got into trouble. It is interesting to see how they reach such a one with a few vigorous strokes, take it to land, up-end it by the heels to let the water run out, and lay it on the grass to dry.

The Snergs dress in tight-fitting woollen hose, with a jerkin of the same material and a leather belt, and little round leather caps rather like the deeper kinds of saucers. When at home most of them live in the town; some few have their mills and farms a little distance away, but they come in pretty often for they are gregarious people, loving company. The town has one main street which goes rambling round corners, with one or two little alleys branching off from it through archways and so forth, and the houses are three or four or more stories in height, built in an irregular way of timber and clay and plaster, top-heavy in appearance though sound in reality even if a bit elastic. If a house leans over more than it should they prop it up by timbers reaching across to the house opposite, this generally giving them an excuse for making a little covered-in passage way on the timbers so that they can visit one another without all the fuss of going downstairs and up again, they being great on visits. You never know when a Snerg will finish with his house because he is always making additions to it, such as throwing out bay windows, or carrying a balcony on stilts to one of the big trees near by and then building a spare bedroom in the tree itself, and the like fool tricks.

They are long-lived people; roughly speaking they live as long as oaks. For instance those Snergs who remember the excitement caused by the landing of

William the Conqueror (1066) are old, old gaffers, opinionated, sitting in arm-chairs. The men who remember the Wars of the Roses are middle-aged and of ripe judgment (in so far as a Snerg ever has judgment), while those born about the time of the Gunpowder Plot have still something of the gay insouciance of youth. The babies date from Trafalgar and upwards.

They are great on feasts, which they have in the open air at long tables joined end on and following the turns of the street. This is necessary because nearly everybody is invited—that is to say, commanded to come, because the King gives the feasts, though each person has to bring his share of food and drink and put it in the general stock. Of late years the procedure has changed owing to the enormous number of invitations that had to be sent; the commands are now understood and only invitations to stay away are sent to the people who are not wanted on the particular occasion. They are sometimes hard up for a reason for a feast, and then the Master of the Household, whose job it is, has to hunt for a reason, such as its being somebody's birthday. Once they had a feast because it was nobody's birthday that day.

The King presides at the head of the table, with the best people on either hand, and there they sit in the mellow evening light and tell tales of the brave days of old and listen to the sound of harps. But at the other end of the table, round the corner and out of sight, there is often a good deal of reckless behaviour and talk, since there is no one to check the number of cups of mead they drink; and the truth is they get slightly tiddleums, and laugh far too much and grab off each other's caps and throw them in other fellow's faces, and so on. Queer people.

The tale is going to start very soon but it will be necessary to give some account of the two children, Sylvia and Joe, who got mixed up with the strange doings I have mentioned, and also of Vanderdecken and his men, because if it had not been for them I really don't know how things would have come out as well as they did. Let us begin with Sylvia.

SYLVIA

Sylvia's mother was a widow who lived in a commodious house in London and who was much admired, and whom we will call Mrs Walker because it was not her name. Though she was rather proud of Sylvia in a way, because she was a pretty little girl with hair that curled naturally, she never bothered about her very much owing to her Society engagements. She never, for example, made her laugh with the business of the little pigs, or pretended to eat her, beginning with the feet, and she never bored people by exhibiting her little frocks to show how she was growing out of them; in fact, she never saw her at all except sometimes when she spared a moment to run upstairs before going to dinners and dances and the like. But she provided a capable nurse called Norah who was skilled in all things necessary for young ones, including interesting tales, and this worked finely until Norah had to go away and marry a young man in the sausage business. The new nurse who came had her own society engagements to attend to (though not such classy ones) and could not spare very much time for Sylvia.

One day Sylvia got wet through in the park and the nurse (Gwendoline) forgot to change her things, so that she got ill. She got more and more ill and the doctor was sent for, but he was absolutely rude to Mrs Walker because he had not been sent for before and this upset her as she was not accustomed to rudeness But what made her more upset was the sight of a dowdy, middle-aged woman who had got in somehow and was sitting by Sylvia's bed, and when she asked her what she was doing there she got no answer but a snort, so she went away. And half an hour later there was a real trouble, for the dowdy person and Sylvia were missing.

There was a good deal of excitement because there had been one or two cases of this kind lately, and there were head-lines in the papers about it; but nothing more happened and the little bed was empty for keeps. In time—that is to say, in three weeks—the matter had blown over, and Mrs Walker went into mourning and looked so absolutely sweet and lovely that Sir Samuel Gollop (Biscuits) asked for her hand and got it and serve him right, and she is now my Lady Gollop, with a house in one of the best parts and two cars and a Pekinese which has taken a prize. But no Sylvia, never again.

And Sylvia was learning to play a new kind of water-polo in which seals take part and was fast forgetting all about her former life except the tales Norah used to tell her.

JOE

Joe is a sturdy boy of about the same age as Sylvia who has caused the Society more anxiety and exasperation than any ten other boys of his weight and size. When he first arrived he was by no means sturdy; his legs and arms were thin, and on all corners of him there was either a bruise or a place breaking out. This was owing to his father, a circus rider, who used to train Joe to do dexterous tricks with ropes and poles so that he would in time be able to earn money and help support the family—which, by the way, now consisted only of Father; his mother had been worn out long ago.

Every time Joe missed doing the tricks dexterously it meant trouble for him, for his father used to drink as much as his wages allowed and this impaired his judgment and led him many times to nearly overdo what he used to do to Joe in the evenings at home. Joe never complained to the other circus people because he believed that boys came into the world for the purpose of being hammered by their parents; also he worked it out that if he did complain his father would do him in as he had often promised to do and, ridiculous as it may seem to us, Joe wanted to go on living.

Matters came to a finish one evening when he had made a deplorable mess of some gymnastics and his father was greatly annoyed with him, and, as he said he would, "put it acrost him" properly. He was interrupted by the sudden appearance of a grim elderly lady bigger than he was, whom he had noticed several times lately in the one-and-threepence seats, and who now burst open his private kitchen door in defiance of the law and picked up the tongs, not by the handle but by the other end. Then Father knew no more for hours.

And when he did know more it was very unsatisfactory. His skull seemed loose like a jig-saw puzzle, and he was in a horrid mess. And Joe was gone. There were no head-lines in the paper about this case because no one cared anything about it—except Father—and by the time his skull was fitted close together again by the great skill of surgeons (his nose they could do nothing with) Joe was becoming justly celebrated among the other children for his reckless way of riding bucking bears bare-backed, and doing other things contrary to regulations.

VANDERDECKEN AND HIS MEN

As the strange adventures of Joe and Sylvia were primarily due to what Joe did to Vanderdecken's crew's soup, it is advisable to give here a short account of these interesting foreigners.

As I have said, Vanderdecken (vulgarly known as the Flying Dutchman) had come in some time before and camped on the bank of a river north of Watkyns Bay. They had had so much tossing about the seas since they started out from Holland in the seventeenth century that it was quite a nice change for them, and they were in no hurry to go away, even though they were very anxious to see their wives and babies again. And it was just as well that they were in no hurry to go, for their wives and babies had all died hundreds of years ago and it would have been a distressing shock to them if they had managed to reach home, this in itself a doubtful matter.

Each man had his hut, made of stout reeds with a roof of palm branches. They stood in a semicircle, with a double-sized one in the middle for Vanderdecken, and there was a garden in front in which was planted some sweet-peas and a few simple bulbs. There was also a large general hut where they had their meals and sat about the table afterwards, smoking their long pipes and talking about how they really must think of getting busy with the old ship and cleaning her up for the voyage. She was in a bad way, with the sails all patched and the carved dolphins on her bows all worn smooth with the seas she had dived into for so many weary years; but the most they ever did towards getting her ready was to lighten her by taking the heavy things out and putting them on shore—quaint old cannon and the two spare anchors, and bales of spices and elephants' tusks, and casks of salt beef all hard as horn from age, and so forth. Each seaman took his chest and hammock ashore and made his hut neat with a floor of little mashed-up shells, and perhaps a shelf or two and a rack for pipes and pannikins and other small matters. Vanderdecken's parrot was still going strong, for the curse had come on him too (not that that troubled him) and he sat on a perch outside in the sun with a tin pot full of nuts beside him, swearing in High Dutch.

It is to be regretted that their relations with the Society, though friendly, were not at all enthusiastic. In the first place, they were, like all Dutchmen, phlegmatic and not given to gush. In the second place, England was at war with Holland when they started out and they did not like the sight of the British flag flying over the main building in Watkyns Bay. It was of course Miss Watkyns' duty to make the first call, so she went with six of the ladies and told them that she had no objection to their staying there—which seemed rather superfluous as they had already settled down very comfortably—and that she hoped they would find the rest and change beneficial. No refreshments were offered, for Vanderdecken had no tea but only Schnapps, a heady liquor calculated to make an unaccustomed man climb trees and therefore obviously unsuited to ladies. The call was returned in due time by Vanderdecken and his mate and two washed seamen; and from then on there were little formal calls at intervals, but, as I say, no real cordiality; mostly talk about the weather.

But the Dutchmen get on famously with the Snergs, who visit them frequently and invite them over to the town for week-ends, this giving a nice excuse for a feast. Then they introduced them to a special kind of mead made from wild bees' honey, with a little distillation of ginger added to give it a kick. This was glad news to the weary mariners, for though they had started out with a good supply of Schnapps they had of course not taken the curse into account and the supply was getting alarmingly low, and there had been many wrinkled brows over the matter. Hunting parties are organized very often; the Dutchmen go with strangely carved muskets and the Snergs with bows and arrows, and they come home with mixed bags. This, however, has caused trouble with the Society, for Miss Watkyns said she could not allow promiscuous slaying of animals in the forest land between the coast and the Snerg country; that if they liked (she meant this ironically) they could go to the country beyond the deep river, where rumour had it there were fierce beasts worthy of their skill, and kill as many as they liked. She gave a list of animals that were prohibited; among these were cinnamon bears, young deer and various sorts of birds. Vanderdecken objected strongly to this, and he came over to argue the matter; but there was breeding in the man and he finally gave way. They now hunt only large deer, hares, duck, and wobsers, a swift-running, graminivorous animal something between a platypus and a pig, but with a prehensile tail. Cooked with bay leaves they are delicious.

But though there was no great cordiality between the ladies of the Society and the Dutchmen, there was no friction to speak of. Miss Watkyns would often send over a few dozen eggs or a basket of plums from the orchard and the like, and Vanderdecken sent one of his men to plant tulips in the way they should be planted, the Dutch being very skilful at this. When the ladies' bathing kiosk blew over in a high wind he and his men came and put it right side up by brute force, and last Christmas he sent two sacks of little carved windmills for the children: On the whole relations could be called satisfactory.

HOW THE ADVENTURE STARTED

Having given a short general statement of conditions, it is now time to recount what happened to Sylvia and Joe owing to her impulsiveness and his disobedience and cheek, and I say again (for it is a point that will bear repetition) that I hope the tale will not be without due effect on my young readers.

I have already said that Joe caused the Society anxiety and exasperation. This was chiefly owing to his insatiable curiosity to know what would be the effect of certain acts, particularly those that were forbidden, and though the lady who was responsible for his arrival (Miss Gribblestone) had lectured him and read him moral tales, such as the one about the boy who was devoured by curiosity and finished by getting devoured by a serpent, and though Miss Watkyns had told him that at his rate of going severe punishment was only a matter of time, all this had little or no effect. And the really serious part was that he and Sylvia were firm chums and she, being impulsive, would aid and abet him in his enterprises.

They could not live apart, these two. They shared everything they had, including secrets, and any little extra snacks that came into their possession. They even shared a puppy (whom they named Tiger owing to his ferocity with slippers and other small matters, and who was pure white all over except on one ear and the left side of the head where he looked as if he had been well rubbed in a tin of blacking) and this is the only known case of dual ownership since Miss Watkyns made that excellent rule of one child, one animal.

Many were the remedies proposed for their improvement, but the difficulty was that the Misses Scadging and Gribblestone could not agree to any particular method. Miss Scadging was the one who had taken Sylvia away from her mother, and she said that Joe had an evil influence on the little girl and that he alone should be punished. Miss Gribblestone on the other hand was of opinion that if it were not for Sylvia's encouragement Joe would be a pattern boy like that Edgar of the story-book who went out before breakfast and gathered fresh groundsel for his aunt's canary. And so the matter stood, for Miss Watkyns made it a rule never to interfere except in very urgent cases.

That Sylvia encouraged the boy there was no doubt. She had blue eyes and a quantity of fluffy gold curls, and consequently, when she giggled and told him he would never dare to do what he said would be a choice thing to do, he usually went at once and did it, whatever it happened to be. And when the deed was done and some of the ladies went forth to pick up the bits or to do whatever else needed doing and to bring in Joe and Sylvia for immediate explanation, they would find them at the time harmless and lovable, perhaps sitting on the shore with their arms round each other's necks as good as gold, or else engaged in some deed of kindness, such as swimming out to the Penguins' Rock with a little string bag full of snails.

HOW IT REALLY BEGAN

To come to how it really began, one bright morning the two went over to Vanderdecken's camp without leave, and there Joe was wicked enough and foolish enough to heave half a brick into the cauldron of soup preparing for the mariners. It was a wicked thing to do because they had never harmed him, and a foolish thing because detection was certain. But he had bragged that he would do it, and Sylvia had giggled in the usual way and said she didn't believe him, so he hunted up the half-brick and off they went.

Speaking of the act entirely apart from its moral aspect I may say that it was a good shot. Six mariners were standing about the cauldron, sniffing the fragrant steam and speaking in praise of the cook, when the missile arrived from a high neighbouring rock, and its impact caused the hot, glutinous liquid to bespatter their faces and clothing. On the next instant Joe, Sylvia and Tiger started home at a brisk run. Arriving breathless they proceeded at once, and in sight of some of the ladies, to be kind to animals. They gathered handfuls of grass and offered them to some overfed sheep, and their expression while doing so was something like that on the faces of angels in the pictures of Murillo, that great painter.

In due time the six mariners and the cook arrived to make their complaint. Their annoyance was so great that, though fluent, they were unintelligible; I am inclined to think that at first they could only articulate expletives in use among Dutch seamen of the seventeenth century. But at length they were calmed sufficiently to enable them to state their case and to demand that Joe, whom they had recognized, be delivered over to them for the punishment of keelihauling, a term which was not understood by any of the ladies.

Miss Watkyns was sympathetic, but she could not, of course, allow them to take the law into their own hands. She soothed them down with diplomatic words, promised that the boy should receive castigation proportional to his offence, and gave them each a ball of some composition warranted to remove grease stains without injuring the fabric.

Then she went for the Handy Encyclopaedia to see what it had to say about keel-hauling. It was as follows:

"Keel-hauling. A form of discipline once in great vogue among seamen. The usual method of application was to attach ropes to the four limbs of the delinquent, lower him over the bows of the ship, and drag him to the stern post and up again, the process being repeated as many times as was considered necessary to expiate the offence. In very serious cases it was the custom to continue the operation until such barnacles as had accumulated on the ship's keel had been scraped off. See Shell Fish."

"I gather that they are vexed," observed Miss Watkyns to herself as she replaced the volume. Then—for in spite of her high ideals she was human—"I should have liked to see that half-brick arriving."

In the conference that followed Miss Scadging proposed that Joe should be considered the sole culprit, since he was a boy and therefore it was his duty to set an example to the weaker sex. Miss Gribblestone objected to this on principle; she was by no means convinced that women were the weaker sex and she recounted again how she had laid out Joe's father; also she quoted Police

Court instances of crimes committed by men at the instigation of females. Miss Watkyns was of opinion that a good and quick way to settle the matter would be to hand Joe six or ten of the very best with the back of a hairbrush before the assembled children; but Miss Gribblestone objected strongly to this as tending to break the boy's spirit. She made the counter-suggestion of an appeal to his pride.

    It is no exaggeration to say that I could keep on like this for pages, but I will not risk wearying the reader with a disquisition on the arguments for and against corporal punishment. I will merely state that it was finally decided to let Sylvia off for just this once, but to incarcerate Joe for the rest of the day in the Turret Chamber on a diet of bread and water.

THE TURRET CHAMBER

The Turret Chamber was, as its name implies, a chamber in a turret. I have previously explained that the erection of the buildings was done by the Snergs; also that their natural tendency was to indulge in wild architectural freaks. By careful watching, however, Miss Watkyns had managed to keep them building according to the neat plans she had prepared, and to subdue their inclination to spoil the symmetry of the houses by fantastic and unnecessary additions. But during her absence one day on a picnic the Snergs broke loose and built a swift tower in a corner of the main building, with some scalloped fancy work on the walls and a twisting flight of stairs in the interior leading to the chamber in question, and by the time she arrived home they were already roofing it in. In appearance it resembled the more despicable forms of lighthouses, and it was quite useless for anything practical, being so narrow that a grown-up person ascending the stairs had to writhe up like a snake, and the chamber atop being so small that Miss Watkyns had considered the question of turning the whole business into a pigeon-house. However, it did very well as a lock-up for Master Joe.

HOW JOE BORE CAPTIVITY

Hours had passed. The sun was not now so very high in the heavens. From the direction of the beach came the sounds of happy shrieks; the children were having a great time there. On the window-sill of the turret chamber sat Joe, his hands in his shorts' pockets and his feet dangling outside, looking forth disconsolately. Behind him on the floor was a platter with odd bits of dry bread, and a pitcher of clear cold water from the pump. There was nothing else behind him but a little wooden bench; the chamber was as bare and smooth as an empty jam-pot. Above him was the bright blue sky. Before him was green grass and waving forest. Below him was a nasty drop of twenty-seven feet. I don't think I have left anything out.

Joe started suddenly and looked about, for from somewhere he had heard the hoot of the Aviola, or small downy owl, which by rights should be still asleep at that hour. He replied with the half-whistle, half-bleat of the Crested Grebe (these were secret signals), and Sylvia came worming her way out from the neighbouring herbaceous border, accompanied by their small but faithful hound. She parted her mass of curls, which had fallen across her face in the passage, and stood having a good look at him.

"Oh, Joe," she said in the low voice of pity, "are you very beastly lonely up there?"

"Yes, Sylvia, I'm just as lonely and miserable! And I've had nothing to eat but some dry bread. I think they dried it on purpose."

"And Tiger's been wondering what's the matter, Joe." She held him up, and Tiger caught sight of Joe and wriggled and made moans, as of a puppy that wanted comfort. "But I've got something for you."

She put down Tiger and produced a handkerchief. "I've got some apple sauce on bits of bread that aren't so dry, and a piece of seedy cake. And some pears. I suppose you haven't got a piece of string?"

"Yes I have," he answered joyfully. "I've got my fishing line. Here it is. I've been fishing for hours and hours trying to fish up something to play with, but all I got was some bits of twigs and I couldn't do much with them."

Sylvia hooked her handkerchief with the provisions on to the line, and a moment later Joe was eating busily.

"You're just like a captive princess in a tower," she said after a time. "Like Rapunzel."

"Except I haven't got such long hair. I feel like an old cat up a pole—except I can't get down. When are they going to let me out?"

"Miss Watkyns said when all of us are in bed. Isn't she vicious?"

"But that's hours and hours! Oh, Sylvia, I must get out!" He bounced up and down on the window-sill, and Sylvia squawked.

"Oh, Joe, you ass, you'll fall!"

"Not me, don't you think it." He bounced up and down again to show his skill.

"Look here, Joe, shall I hook on Tiger? I'll tie him in my hankie so that he won't fall and then you can play with him for a bit—No, you keep him up there with you, and then won't Miss Watkyns be surprised when she finds him there! She'll think he's got wings somehow."

"Yes, that'd be fine. But I've got a much better idea, Sylvia. You just bring me that clothes-line over there."

"What for? And it's got nighties drying on it."

"I don't want them, I want only the rope. Do, Sylvia, it's something delicious. If you don't I'll show you how to hang out of a window head downwards."

"No, don't!" cried Sylvia. "I'll bring it." She ran off and came back a minute later with the clothes-line, which she fastened to his fish-hook. "Nighties all over the grass. There'll be a fine row over it if they catch me. You are a headstrong boy, Joe."

Joe did not answer, for he was busy. He hauled up the rope and fastened one end of it to the bench, and then managed to jam the bench across the window frame. Then he called to Sylvia to stand from under.

"Because," he said, "it's rather a rotten piece of rope, and besides, I don't think this silly old bench is going to stand much jerking about. But we'll soon see."

On the next instant, Sylvia gave a screech, for there was Joe outside the window, spinning round on the rope. But before you could count ten he had slid down to the ground and Tiger was leaping and trying to get at his face so as to lick it. Not a very wonderful trick for a circus boy, but then Sylvia didn't know anything about circuses. She put her arms round his neck and hugged him.

"Oh, Joe," she said, "you are a brave boy! You looked just like a clean monkey coming down—except that you haven't got a tail. But how are you going to get the rope put back?"

"I'm not bothering about the rope," said Joe. "You see we're just going to run away."

"Run away! What for?"

"For fun. I'm not going to be locked up by anybody. I'm going over to see the Snergs, and you've got to come with me. Tiger's coming, too, of course. We'll have a glorious time!"

"What do you mean, you contentious infant?" (She sometimes used words she had heard from Miss Watkyns and other ladies.) "It's miles and miles and miles! And you don't know the way there."

"Yes I do. It's straight over there, just a little bit this side of where the sun goes under. We'll just go that way until we can't see it, and then we'll sleep in a nice place in the forest."

"Yes, Clever, and what about to-morrow? The sun's always over the sea in the morning."

"Then all we've got to do is to go the other way. Can't you see?"

Sylvia was rather impressed by his resourcefulness. "Yes, but what about afterwards, Joe," she said after a moment. "What will Miss Watkyns do when she knows about it?"

"Yes, but what happens afterwards will happen afterwards. Can't you see? Come along, Sylvia, its adventures, like those tales your nurse told you about. And it's much better being a tale than just hearing it. We'll sleep in the forest to-night-it's nice and warm—and to-morrow sometime we'll be at the Snerg's place and have a jolly time with them. Just think what the other kids will think of us. Won't they be jealous!"

How it happened Sylvia could never quite make out, but she found herself running along hand-in-hand with Joe over the soft turf, with Tiger bouncing alongside of them and sometimes tumbling over his own barks, drawing nearer and nearer to the trees which looked so cool and inviting on that warm afternoon.

"Oh, Joe," she panted as she ran, "what an absurd mite you are!"

THE FOREST LAND

It seemed to these precocious infants that the forest was deeper and shadier and more silent, and the grass softer than they had ever known it before; but perhaps that was because before they had always gone with troops of young ones, which would at least do away with the quietness. In parts where the trees were not so very thick the grass was all dappled with spots of sun, and sometimes there were great shafts of light through the trees to make a guide for them, for all they had to do so far was to go as fast as they could in the direction of the sun. And they ran on and on and on, with the pretence idea that they were fleeing from enemies who knew no touch of mercy and they must get as far as possible while they could.

At length they had to stop running and walk, but they walked hard because Joe said they must keep on for hours and hours. But it was not so very long before they had to sit down and rest, for they were all hot and sticky and getting very hungry. Joe opened Sylvia's handkerchief, in which he carried the rest of the pears she had brought. There were five left, rather soft with the jolting, being ripe, but they ate them, squashed parts and peel and all, and then they had a draught from a stream, lying down on their stomachs and drinking like hunters. Tiger's share of the meal was as much water as he liked to drink, and the sight of him sitting up and thinking after this meagre diet brought into Sylvia's head an idea that perhaps they had been a tiny bit rash. But Joe said that Tiger could make up for it to-morrow by a good blow-out, entirely omitting to consider the many weary miles that lay between them and the country of the Snergs and the slim chance they had of ever finding their way there at all. He said it was really adventures, like the one her nurse had told her of, and he pointed out how very likely it was that something exciting would happen at any moment. Sylvia gave her opinion that they were rather too small to be of much use if anything exciting did occur and said she hoped it wouldn't. She asked him if he thought it would be cold when the dark came, and he said, "No, only nice and cool," for he was an optimist always.

They got up and went on again, following the gleam of the sun as well as they could, until at last it went altogether and they could only see a red glow from the open parts where there were mostly bushes. And still they went on and on and on, until Sylvia said her legs began to feel all wobbly and she had to sit down. There it was: those silly things were deep in the lonely woods and the shadows were creeping up from the far places.

Joe climbed a tree to see if he could see something worth seeing, such as the smoke from an honest wood-cutter's hut or the like, as in the tales of forests; though really he hadn't much expectation of finding anything, for he had been told there was little else but billions of trees between the sea and the Snerg country. All he could see was a little speck of red which he said might be the last of the sunset, or might be a fire made by Indians or cannibals; though of course he did not mean the last part nor did Sylvia believe it or take any interest in it. What she wanted was a bite of real supper and a bed; the forest had been growing darker and more serious and a little shiver went through her as if a lot of the fun had suddenly gone.

"It's getting more and more like one of those tales," said Joe in a satisfied way—as will have been seen, he had a good deal of what is known as the bulldog breed in him. "Specially that part over there where it's like a dark passage. Suppose an old witch was to come along there, flop, flop, flop, and tell us to go home with her."

"Oh, don't, Joe! We don't want it too much like those tales. It's getting awfully lonely. I wish I hadn't come."

"But it's only lonely enough to be nice, Sylvia. Besides, it's great fun. There's nobody to tell us we mustn't do things, or to tell us when to go to bed. We jolly well go to bed when we like."

"Yes, but where are we to go to bed?"

"Oh, somewhere or other. I know! We'll get some fallen leaves, like in the babes in the wood, and cover ourselves up."

"But it's summer time and there aren't any fallen leaves."

"More there are. Then what we've got to do is to cuddle up close. I'll look after you, never fear, and if any old witch was to——" here he stopped suddenly and looked round at the deepening shadows.

"Oh, Joe!" cried Sylvia, getting close up to him and rather behind him.

The sound they heard was a nasty, soft, flopping sound, and it came from the part which Joe had said looked like a dark passage. He wished he had brought a sword with him somehow, or a bow and arrows, or else one of old Vanderdecken's guns even if it did knock him over backwards as the one did that he got hold of one day (but nobody found out who it was). Alas, he had nothing but his wooden scalping knife; but he got it out because it seemed better than nothing.

Then, to the surprise and joy of these infants, a great cinnamon bear hove in sight and came up to them, wagging his head from side to side, and, so to speak, gently barging at them. It took some time to prove to him that they were in no mood for play, but by dint of strenuous pushing at him on one side he got it into his thick head that they wanted him to lie down, and he flopped over. Then they got close up to him, Sylvia on the inside so as to give her as much of the fur as possible, and Tiger curled up in a little hollow space by her neck; and they were soon asleep, for they were very tired, what with the long tramp and the novelty of everything. But what a change! From their nicely prepared supper of warm milk and rusks to cold pears and water. From their clean, decorously tinted dormitory to the lonely wind-sighing forest. From their little cots, with clean sheets spread over resilient aromatic hops, to the lee-side of a bear. And the bear had bad dreams and kept waking them up by moaning and shuddering sounds, and more than once he turned over, forgetting all about them, and Joe had to punch him and pull his fur hard to let him know that there were young folks and a puppy underneath. It was a long, hard, disagreeable night, and they were right glad when, after a week as it seemed, the dawn came.

THE DAWN

There was nothing special about the dawn when it did come. It was cold and grey and shivery, with a mist that hid the trees a little distance away, and Sylvia felt very discontented and hungry and really wished she hadn't listened to Joe. He on the other hand was very brave and strong, and he rubbed her hands and feet to warm them and then turned somersaults backwards to warm himself; to the great surprise of the bear, who sat up on his hind legs and stared, as cinnamons will at anything new. There was nothing to eat except some chilly berries all covered with dew, and these did not appeal to the children's stomachs at that hour. But the bear ate large quantities of them and they had to kick him to make stop stuffing and come on.

Joe helped Sylvia on to the bear's back, and she sat there with Tiger clasped to her because he was now a very silent pup owing to his having had nothing to eat for such a long time, and they went on their way for some miles—that is to say, they went on in an opposite, direction to where they could see signs of sunrise over the trees. But the bear did not understand that they wanted him to go as near due west as possible, and he kept turning up sylvan glades at right angles and Joe had continuously to push his head round in the way he should go.

They parted with him suddenly and in a surprising way. He caught sight of a hollow tree in the middle distance, from which issued bees in large numbers though peacefully, and he intimated by grunts that there was food for all hands and to spare. Before they quite realized what he meant he was charging up to the tree, and Sylvia had just time to slip from his back. In another instant he was tearing away at the rotten part of the tree to get at the honey, and clouds of bees came out in a horrible rage to see about it. Joe caught Sylvia's hand and dragged her into a clump of bushes just in time, and they went tearing through it and then as hard as they could pelt over the grass until they were a long way off. They could hear, subdued by distance, the hum of bees like the rich deep note of a church organ, and the mixed grunting and howling of the bear; though whether the latter sounds were those of joy or grief was a doubtful question. Sylvia said that bears did not feel pain from bees' stings except on the tip of the nose because their fur protected them, but Joe was of opinion that they got stung furiously all over but that they considered the honey was worth the pain, hence the mixed quality of the howls.

They went on and on and on, and at last the sun got up and sent beams of cheerful light through the leaves and drove away the mist, so that Sylvia began to feel much better, though hungry, and hungrier as time went on. And just when the question of breakfast had become a really serious and mournful subject, they roused a shout of joy, for they saw coming towards them down the woodland ways one Gorbo, a Snerg.

GORBO THE SNERG

Gorbo was a well-known, utterly irresponsible Snerg who occasionally came over to Watkyns Bay to do a job of work, and who was quite celebrated for his habit of doing it very badly and getting tired of it almost at once and wandering off again. He was of average size for a Snerg and fairly young—possibly two hundred and fifty—and though good-natured to excess he had little intelligence of the useful kind. He had given it out that he was a potter by trade—he had indeed some superficial knowledge of the business—and he had induced Miss Watkyns to let him start a little kiln in order to supply the Society with pots. But there was no particular shape to his pots when he had made them and many of them fell to bits when they were handled, so Miss Watkyns told him plainly that he was a fraud; and to this he agreed heartily for he did not like to contradict people. She told him to go away—to potter off was her bitter expression—so he had gone to spend a day or two with Vanderdecken's men, who rather liked his face but I don't know why, and then he had come across the forest on his way to the town, where he had a little house of one room and a kitchen. And that is why the children met him that morning, grinning all over his face and carrying his bow and arrows, and a little bundle containing his few potter's tools and his other shirt and a bunch of wheat-cakes. He had slept in a thicket of ferns, some of which he had chopped up to form a sort of nest, and what with the odds and ends of fern sticking to his clothes and his wild hair straggling out from his saucer cap, he looked as disreputable a person as you might expect to meet even among the Snergs, who are not over particular about their personal appearance at the best.

But he was a welcome sight to Sylvia and Joe. All three took hands and made two little dancing steps first to one side and then to the other, which is the Snerg manner of greeting, and which all the children had taken to (in spite of Miss Watkyns' objection to it as absurd and unnecessary) and he was then asked if he had anything to eat. He produced his wheat-cakes and then made a little fire in order to warm them up on his potter's trowel, which he cleaned first with a bunch of grass. Before they sat down to eat he sneaked up to a herd of deer which came into sight a little distance away and somehow blarneyed one of them into letting him milk her. He came back with a good deal of milk in a silver-tipped horn that he had, and the children divided it between them. They did not reflect of course that they were causing some small deer to go short that morning. But it was a very jolly breakfast. It was quite a joy to the children to note Tiger's figure showing signs of sleekness and roundness again; he being of an age when it shows quickly.

When Gorbo heard that they had the nerve to run away he was not at all shocked at their folly but highly delighted with their sporting character, which is just what would be expected of him. But he said it was lucky they had met him, because left to themselves it was very doubtful if they would ever reach the town; and there was always the danger that they might wander into the parts where the trees grew closer and closer and are all twisted until at last there is no going forwards or backwards, and then they would be lost for keeps and a fine to-do. This, by the way, is the only thing with a touch of sense in it that he ever said to them, on that day at least.

Feeling tremendously refreshed with this wholesome meal, they started off again on their journey, Gorbo leading the way and showing nice little short-cuts through clumps of bracken and so forth, and sometimes carrying Sylvia over rough ground and through swampy places and the like. They had the luck to meet another large cinnamon bear, which carried both children for several miles; but at length it intimated in the usual way that it had had enough (this is done by crouching on the ground with all four paws tucked underneath, laying the head sideways, and emitting a long, loud, melancholy howl). So they got off and the bear sprang up and went swiftly away, and they never found another. It was the time of the annual migration of bears to the country of slug-nuts, and that is why so few bears were seen on this trip.

It was a long journey and both children got very tired; Gorbo had at last to carry Sylvia pick-a-back, while Joe had to carry the puppy, who was getting his pads sore with so much travel. But just when it seemed to them that there would never be any end to the journey, to their great joy they saw from a slight eminence a cluster of high-peaked red roofs, which Gorbo told them (rather unnecessarily I think) was the town.

THE TOWN

As none of the children had ever been seen in the town before, the arrival of Joe and Sylvia was the signal for a good deal of fuss and feathers. Snergs rushed out of their houses into the street and swarmed on the roofs and climbed about, and babies were held on high so that they might see. Some clever ones rushed to the town belfry and rang a peal, others got busy with strips of coloured cloth and had them rigged across the street in no time. The four brightest got out the town drums and went to meet them.

The crowd became dense, and considerate persons shouted "Stand back! Give them air!" Joe and Sylvia felt rather shy and uncomfortable at all the display, but Gorbo stepped out proudly for he was beginning to think this was a far, far better thing than he had ever done. And so, amid the shouts of the populace, with music before them, they went up the street.

Gorbo was full of hope that the King would see great merit in this his doing and that he would get a decoration for it. Nearly everybody had one of some sort or another, and though he did not go so far as to expect one of the best he hoped he would at least get the Order of the Brazen Nutmeg. He was soon undeceived. The Master of the Household came up to him with a stern look and bade him follow him to the King's presence and explain what was his little game. Then he gave a hand to each of the children and led them to the Royal House.

THE ROYAL HOUSE

The Royal House is the only building in the town that stands without being propped up by another building, and naturally this gives it an imposing appearance. Picture to yourself columns of quaintly carved oak surrounding an audience chamber on the ground floor and supporting the spreading-out part of the stories above. On the first floor are the private apartments, the dining-hall (with a sufficient minstrel's gallery giving elbow room for four minstrels to perform the most energetic pieces) and the room where the regalia is kept in a padded box. On the floor above live the Court officials, three of them, and on the third or attic floor, are rooms for the domestic staff and one large room containing odd matters that are bound to collect in any large household, such as chairs wanting a leg, damaged pieces of armour, swords with loose hilts, old pairs of bellows, and the like. The kitchen is in another building, connected to the dining-hall by an overhead passage which is covered in so that the victuals will not get chilled on the way. Altogether a neat and commodious dwelling for a king in a small way of business.

THE KING OF THE SNERGS

The King, Merse II, was quite an agreeable looking man, with the typical chubby face of the Snergs framed in a fringe of black whiskers that resembled chinchilla. He was fully four feet in height, broad and inclined to stoutness. He bade the children be seated on either side of him and spoke to them kindly, hoping that they were not too tired with the journey and inquiring politely after the health of Miss Watkyns and the other ladies. Joe and Sylvia were rather shy but very pleased; it now seemed to them that they had acted quite wisely in making this absurd expedition.

Then the King turned to Gorbo, who stood cap in hand, still holding on to his bundle and other matters. I will endeavour to give as literal a translation of the talk as possible.

"Hail, Gorbo, cleverest and brightest of the Snergs we don't think," said the King.

"Hail, King. May your shadow be ever a wide one." (This is the formal reply to a Royal salutation.)

"And what doest thou here with these young ones, O Ornament to the race the other way round?"

"I met them in the woodland, O King," replied Gorbo, now getting very nervous.

"Yes. And in what part of that wide address didst thou find them, thou first-class brain perhaps not?"

"Er—just this side of Toadstool Hollow, O King."

"Ha! And had'st thou, thou nimble lout, any hand in inducing them to wander further from their home?"

Gorbo went down upon his knees, as a good safe position. "No, O King, not at all. They said they were coming here, so I—I showed them the way."

"Excellent! And it did not occur to thee, thou farthing rascal, to lead them back to their little home by the sea?"

"N—no, O King, I-I didn't think."

"That we believe, thou worse than worm."

The King crossed his legs and meditated, with his chin resting on his hand. "And what," he asked at length, turning to Joe, "will Miss Watkyns (on whom be peace) think of these thy wanderings?"

"I don't know, O King," replied Joe, hoping he was saying it correctly. "We just scooted. For fun," he added to make it sound more reasonable.

"For fun, sayest thou, small man! And had'st thou wandered with this golden-haired babe into parts where the trees are locked like twisted serpents and there is no light, wouldst thou then have found thy fun?"

Joe wriggled and felt horribly uncomfortable. The King then turned to the Master of the Household, who was standing by the kneeling Gorbo, contemptuously snipping at his ears.

"And what thinkest thou of this strange matter?" he asked.

"I think," replied the officer, "that it were a good excuse for a feast."

"Excellently said!" exclaimed the King. "So be it. We will first dispatch fleet messengers to Miss Watkyns to calm her fears, and then celebrate the visit of these tiny ones" (they were nearly as tall as he was) " by a banquet of the best. But," he added, pointing the finger of scorn at Gorbo, "give to this all but black-beetle a courteous loving invitation to stay away from it."

"Please, O King," began Sylvia timidly. Then she stopped suddenly, for everybody had turned to look at her.

"Speak on, pretty one," said the King, encouragingly, laying his hand upon her curls. "What hair!"

"Please it wasn't Gorbo's fault," went on Sylvia. "You see—er—O King, Joe and I ran away—for fun—and Gorbo found us when we were hungry and he gave us lots to eat. And he got some milk from a deer for us, and found us a bear to ride part of the way."

"Gorbo's a jolly good sort, O King," added Joe.

"Oh, then that alters the case," said the King briskly. (He was rather impulsive). "Rise, Gorbo. We cancel the invitation and command you to feast with us this day—but not too near us. The safe arrival of these little ones across the forest," he added in a general way to everybody, "together with the discovery of a gleam of sense in that varlet, make this indeed a day of strange happenings."

Sylvia and Joe were then taken charge of by the Queen, a fat, smiling person who came into the audience chamber at this point. They had first a good wash, and then a toothsome little snack of bean fritters mixed with honey, and a cup of milk, to carry on with until the time of the feast, and Tiger had a large plate of bread sop with meat in it, after which he went to sleep for hours. While they were eating the Queen came with a comb and fluffed out Sylvia's hair and put some fancy extra curls in it. Then, after a little rest, they went to watch the preparations outside.

It was an interesting sight. The people had not had a feast for more than a week and it came as a welcome change. Men were staggering about with tables and joining them end on in the proper way, and placing stools and benches in position. There were 38 tables altogether and each one was about 12 feet long—

38×12=456 feet—so you will see that a noble spread it was going to be; it reached from the Royal House to as far as beyond the market-place. From every kitchen came the smell of savoury baked meats. At the open windows little stout women could be seen rolling out pastry. Grave, responsible Snergs measured the mead into jars and placed them at the proper intervals on the tables. Harpers put new strings to their harps. The Court jester went to his attic and got out a little secret volume from beneath the mattress and mugged up some merry jests.

THE FEAST

At the appointed hour horns sounded and all sat down to table in the calm evening light. At the head were the King and Queen, side by side. To the right and left sat Sylvia and Joe, and after them came the best people, then the ordinary Snergs in order of importance. At the extreme end of the table, somewhere in the suburbs, sat Gorbo. That's what they thought of him.

I am happy to report that the Queen kept a careful watch on what the two children ate or else there might have been serious trouble for them later, the food being of a very grown-up sort. They were given each a very tiny mug of mead and she told them to go slow with it. (The Snerg youngsters, by the way, can put away an imperial pint and still behave. Use is everything). It was all very jolly for them to find themselves treated with so much pomp and circumstance, and they felt that they had some glorious things to tell the other kids when they arrived home. There occurred one unfortunate incident, however, which helped to reduce any tendency towards swelled heads. They had heard before that the Snergs considered it shocking bad form to feed dogs when at table—every race has its own peculiar ideas on behaviour—but when two nice friendly dogs, rather like retrievers, came one on each side of Sylvia and watched every mouthful that she took, she was greatly tempted to give them a bit, especially as their mouths watered so much that she could actually hear the drips. It was when one of them began a gentle moaning sound that she could stand it no longer, so just when she thought the King and Queen were looking the other way she slipped a piece of meat into his mouth. He snapped it up and lashed the floor with his tail; the other dog instantly sprang up and put two paws on her lap and gazed into her eyes. In an instant all the talk had stopped and everybody stared at her.

It was a horrible moment, and she became crimson. But the King came to her aid with true politeness. He cut a piece of knuckle end of lamb and flung it to his favourite hound, and the situation was saved. (The Prince of Wales, I believe, once took a good swig out of his finger-bowl to put an unpolished guest at his ease.) But it was necessary to have all dogs removed after this, as they came crowding up, full of hope.

There was some good music from harps, and the jester asked some clever riddles, one of which was new. A young Snerg who had a really fine tenor voice sang, "Give me thy gold, I ask no more," very movingly. But perhaps the most delightful (though slightly embarrassing) moment was when, at a given signal, the whole push stood up and drained a cup of mead to "Our Guests."

The declining sun shone round a corner of the street; the scene was now in mellow light and shade. Snergs began to loll against each other and reach lazily for the nut-crackers. From the end of the table, 486 feet away, came shouts of unseemly mirth: Gorbo, that ass, had made a bet that he would stand on his head on a pyramid of mead pots, and the crash was terrific. The King sent a stern word that there was to be not so much of it. The sudden discovery that Joe and Sylvia were both sound asleep in their little arm-chairs caused no particular break in the proceedings. They were carried to the Royal House by motherly old Snergs and tucked up in bed, and the feasting and joviality went on.

A MORNING WALK

Will it be thought by the readers at this point that the promised moral lesson is long in coming? It is not improbable. So far I have chronicled a comparatively glorious result of the two children's mutinous behaviour. They had arrived safely, after a journey which, though tiring, was full of interest, and had been received, dined, and wined in the manner of foreign potentates, and to their simple minds it seemed that all they had to do now was to go comfortably home and brag about it. But read on; the moral lesson is coming.

It was one of the quaint old customs of the Snergs to rise an hour or two later on the day after a feast. Consequently, when Joe and Sylvia woke up refreshed and happy, and with none of the sense of guilt befitting children who had wantonly run away from wise and kind rule, they found the whole place very quiet, the only sounds being those of swallows outside the open lattice of their room, and from the adjoining room (the Royal bedchamber), two different kinds of snores.

They crept downstairs and found a smiling old female person sifting cinders outside the kitchen door, and they asked her if she could please tell them when breakfast would be ready. She said it would not be for a long time but she could get them something to help them wait, and she took them into the kitchen and gave them each a warm cake, rather like a rusk only softer, and some milk. They talked about whales, in which she was much interested for she had never seen the ocean; few of the female Snergs ever travel.

They went for a walk down the deserted street and suddenly, in the paved yard where the pump is, they saw Gorbo. He had just soused his head and was drying it on a little coarse towel. They greeted joyfully and sat down on three buckets that happened to be there and talked of the news while Gorbo combed his wild head with a piece of comb that he had.

The news was this. A Snerg messenger had come on the run from Miss Watkyns late in the evening, saying that they had disappeared and would the King please turn all hands out at once to hunt for them, taking something to eat and a bottle of milk in case. Vanderdecken's men in the meantime were ranging along the seashore, poking into caverns and places to see if they could find them, and sweeping the horizon for anything new, such as a raft flying the black flag—for they believed almost anything possible of Joe. Apparently there was great trouble and excitement over the matter at Watkyns Bay, and both children were very proud to be the cause of it all. They would be; they were just that kind.

Of course, as the fleet messengers dispatched by the King must have arrived and calmed Miss Watkyns' fears by this time, there was no need to bother any more, and it had been arranged that Joe and Sylvia were to leave some time after breakfast on two domestic bears, with an escort of six Snergs who would carry four small blankets, two pillows, a kettle, a frying-pan, and some provisions; all these of course because they would have to spend the night in the forest. Joe felt rather upset that the adventures were coming to an end, but Sylvia was pleased. She had had a good deal of fun out of the trip and she felt it would be nice to get back again and be pardoned and petted in due course and tell all the other kids what a riotous time they had had.

They went for a walk with Gorbo across some fields, with Tiger careering ahead of them, for his long rest had done his paws good and he was feeling refreshed and full of prunes. Gorbo pointed out various objects of interest, such as the mill that belonged to his half-brother, and the hillside where the last dragon was killed, long ago when he was a tiny fellow. He remembered quite well some men rushing back and calling out "More arrows! More arrows!" when they had the dragon badly wounded and unable to fly, and how they went dashing back with the fresh supply of arrows and all shot at it until it looked like a pincushion and they could get near enough to stick it with spears and finish it. More than a hundred Snergs lost their lives on that occasion. He was too young to remember the fierce fights that took place when a wandering band of Kelps (possibly a corruption of Kelpies) came through the country, setting fire to the woods and robbing and slaying, but he took them on to rising ground and showed them the dark line that crossed the trees a mile or so away and which marked the deep river, and pointed out more or less the spot where the last battle had been fought. The Kelps had made a stand on a high rock, but the Snergs had gone solidly for them and pierced them with showers of arrows and cut them to bits with swords and pitched the rest into the river. And that, as Gorbo said, was that.

    The most interesting feature of the forest land, he said, was the region of twisted trees, which reached to within a short distance of the town. It was not healthy to go too far in among these trees, but if they liked he would show them a few just on the outskirts, as breakfast wouldn't be ready for at least another hour. The children were delighted at the chance of seeing these strange natural objects, so off they went into the woods.

THE TWISTED TREES

It did not take long to reach the spot where the first few twisted trees were growing. They were wonderful things, with thick smooth grey trunks and smooth grey branches that touched the ground here and there like great quiet serpents. Leaves grew only on the higher parts, but they were thick and matted like a thatch and made it rather dark and creepy underneath. Gorbo led them along to where there were more and much better specimens of this wonderful flora, and Sylvia and Joe were proud that they of all the children had had a chance of seeing them.

Gorbo said it was time to get back and he turned and led the way. Suddenly he stopped and looked about under the writhing grey branches and over them; then he turned in another direction. Again he stopped, and this time he had a particularly silly smile.

"I'd better be careful," he said, "or we'll get lost."

He went on again and the children followed him, hoping that he would find the way out soon, as breakfast was a thing they wanted quickly. But it was getting dark; the sky was now hidden by a roof of matted leaves, and on all sides and above them the thick smooth branches twisted and crossed and locked together. The air was damp and smelt of mould and old moss, and there was a horrid silence. A great leather-skinned bat flickered past them, almost brushing against Sylvia's hair, so that she ducked and gave out a little squeal.

Gorbo at last swarmed up one of the bigger trees and, after a lot of struggling, managed to force his way out through, the leaves, disturbing numbers of bats that came flopping and wheeling about. Joe had to put his arms round Sylvia's head and hide it as well as he could until the foul things had gone to settle elsewhere. A minute or two later, Gorbo came sliding down.

"It's all right," he said. "I couldn't see much else but leaves, but I saw the sun so I know which way to go now. The sun is just over"—here he stopped and thought and scratched his head. "Yes, I think it's over that way. You see I got twisted round a bit coming down."

They followed him again, working their way over and under the branches. After a time he stopped and thought again, and then began climbing and creeping in another direction—it was all climbing and creeping now. Then he stopped and looked at them in dismay. The horrible writhing grey trunks surrounded them on all sides like an ugly giant net, in a gloom so deep that their shapes were lost to the eye a dozen yards away. Gorbo, the clever one, the woodsman, had done this thing. They were lost.

He did not look at them for long; the sight of Sylvia's scared face as she crept from under one of the grey limbs roused him up.

"It's all right, Sylvia," he said. "They'll find we're missing, and this is the first place they'll look for us in. You see they'll start shouting and yelling, and then we'll start shouting and yelling and work our way to where we hear them. It's quite easy. But won't the King go for me! No Brazen Nutmeg for poor old Gorbo. There's a little bigger space over there; let's go and see if we can find a place to sit down comfortably."

They worked their way on, and sure enough there was a little space ahead that was more open owing to there being a huge tree which had, so to speak, pushed all smaller ones out of its way. It was gloomy enough, but there was at least room to stand upright and move about if they felt like it.

"Look!" said Sylvia and Joe suddenly, both together.

Gorbo turned and then stared. In the big tree was a door about four feet high, a queer looking door with mighty iron hinges and clasps, all red with rust or green with moss. In the deep shadow and at a little distance away it was difficult to distinguish it from the trunk.

Gorbo scratched his head and continued to stare. "I've never heard of any door," he said at length. "The Kelps never made any door; they hadn't sense enough; all biting and screaming and killing, I've heard. And it's ever so much too small for Golithos."

"Who's Golithos?" asked Joe quickly.

"Golithos' an ogre," replied Gorbo, truthfully, but like the silly fool he was. Sylvia gave a scream and clutched hold of Joe.

"It's all right, Sylvia," said Gorbo in a hurry. "He was an ogre, but he's not now. He's reformed. Besides, he's been on the other side of the river for ever so long. Don't be frightened."

He went to the door and gave a good pull at a great iron knob. The door swung open quite easily. He poked his head inside.

"Very dark and smells of cheese," he said after a moment.

He went in a little way. "No, it's not quite dark; there's a light coming from somewhere. There's a little flight of steps going down. Come and look."

Joe picked up Tiger and, taking Sylvia by the hand, stepped with her inside the door.

"See," said Gorbo, "there's the steps. Shall we go down and see what we can see?"

"Yes," said Joe eagerly. "Let's!"

"N—n—no," said Sylvia at the same time. "I don't like it."

"Anyway," went on Gorbo, "we'll make sure that the door doesn't shut behind us. I'll push it wide open and then——"

He did not finish what he was going to say, for the door had gently closed. He flung himself furiously at it, but, strong as he was, made no more impression on it than if it had been a stone wall.

Gorbo, that lout, had really done it this time.

PART II

TROUBLE AT WATKYNS BAY

Bitter was the grief and deep the perplexity of Miss Watkyns and all the ladies when news came by other fleet messengers that Sylvia and Joe had disappeared again, and this time in a quite unaccountable way. A little while later King Merse II himself came to Watkyns Bay and explained how bands of responsible Snergs had been sent to explore everywhere and especially in the region of twisted trees, taking with them little sacks of lime to mark their trails, and how they had shouted and yelled until they were hoarse, but without avail, since no answer had come from anywhere, and they had returned home with sore hearts and sore throats. He tried to cheer them up by saying that the children would certainly be found in time, but he did not say anything about his real fear, which was that they had somehow got mixed up with one or other of the magic snares which, tradition had it, were very plentiful among the twisted trees. He quoted old sayings to comfort them, such as it is best not to meet trouble half-way, and that care killed the cat when there was really nothing amiss with the animal. He added that as Providence looked after fools there was cause for cheerful hopes, since Gorbo was the biggest fool even among the Snergs, who, though having many good qualities, are not celebrated for brain waves.

These kind efforts had some effect in restoring confidence and the ladies were able to discuss the matter with comparative calm. Miss Gribblestone had at first wondered whether by some untoward combination of chances the children had slipped back to the scene of their former life, and she drew a pathetic picture of Sylvia and Joe wandering about the streets of London with bare legs and only slinkers on their feet, and possibly starving, and she suggested the advisability of her instant departure for London with a bundle of warm underthings and two woolly coats. Miss Watkyns reproved her with some sharpness, pointing out the impossibility of such a thing: leaving out fifty other reasons the moon was only a quarter full and the air currents would be in opposition, and this alone made the suggestion absurd. Miss Scadging advanced an even wilder theory that the children had suffered such mental anguish from the reproof and punishment given that they had wandered away and died of broken hearts, and at this Miss Watkyns begged her to consider the extravagance of such a suggestion applied to either Sylvia or Joe and to give her energies to a more practical solution of the problem.

When the rest of the children heard the news they were slightly awe-struck but not immoderately grieved, for their experience of Joe and Sylvia had led them to believe they were capable of coming safely out of any trouble, and the general opinion was that they were having a continuation of their surprising and interesting adventures somewhere and would return in due time, full of glory and slightly swollen headed. Poor things, they knew little of the harsh, real world; they had forgotten what happened to them in the past; as has been said, the air of the place was grand for forgetting.

The King next went over to see Vanderdecken and had a long conference with him, and then returned across the forest with his retinue. He had left word with Miss Watkyns that he and a band of picked men would leave next day on an expedition, but for the present he preferred not to say where to, in order to avoid raising either fears or hopes. On his arrival at the town he made a short speech, and then personally superintended preparations. Swords and axes were sharpened, quivers were stuffed with arrows, steel casques had old dents knocked out, cuirasses had the buckles put in order, provisions were packed into little wallets. The air smelt of war, as in the brave days of old.

Miss Watkyns, pacing with knitted brow on her verandah, was disturbed by the sound of shrieks and expletives. Looking up in anger, she saw Vanderdecken and all his men coming up the path, the foremost seaman bearing the parrot's cage—this accounting for the noise, for the bird was enraged. All had their seaboots on, and they bore muskets, powder—horns, pouches with slugs and bullets, cutlasses and snickersnees; each man had also a bag containing pickled beef, biscuits, a cake of tobacco, and a small bottle of Schnapps. Vanderdecken said that they were going away for an indefinite period and asked Miss Watkyns if she would kindly give an eye to the camp in their absence and see that things were aired occasionally and the weeds kept down in the garden. Also, if it was not too much trouble, would she see to it that the Snergs did at least half an hour's pumping of the old ship every morning and evening. He then handed over the parrot with a request that it be supplied with nuts and fruit, and a bit of sulphur in its water to prevent it getting scaly feet, and begged her to pardon any of its verbal lapses. She agreed readily to these requests. and they departed across the forest and joined King Merse and his men on the following morning. An hour later they were all trooping together over the hillside beyond the town.

BEYOND THE DOOR

While Gorbo was battering himself against the heavy little door, which had closed so gently and firmly as if pushed to from without, Sylvia clung to Joe and hid her face and trembled. Joe held her tight without speaking; he, too, tough and adventurous as he was, had received a shock.

Gorbo turned round at last, and in the faint light that came from somewhere below they could see a badly scared look on his face, and it was all twisted as if he were going to cry. He was thinking of the horrid mess he had got the little ones into.

"I've done it this time," he said. "So the old woman was right after all."

"Which old woman?" asked Joe.

"An old woman who told my mother that she would only have one son and that he would be the biggest fool among the Snergs."

"Then it isn't your fault," said Joe, to comfort him. "If it was all settled before you were born."

"That's so!" exclaimed Gorbo. "I must be a fool not to think of that before. But then if I had thought of it," he added mournfully, "I wouldn't be a fool and the old woman would have been wrong; so it works out all right."

"But you're sometimes quite sensible," said Joe. "Isn't he, Sylvia?"

"Y—y—yes," agreed Sylvia. "But I wish we could get out."

"It seems to me," said Gorbo "—not that I am much of a man to listen to—that we should see what we can see down these steps."

"Well, we can't stay here for ever," said Joe, "so let's go."

"I'll go ahead," said Gorbo. "If there are any fierce things that bite below, they can have first bite at me and serve me right."

With this cheerful remark he started off. Joe went next and Sylvia came close behind him. The way was very narrow and so low that their heads nearly touched the roof, small as they were. And they went down and down and down, and the more they went down the lighter it got with a sickly yellowish-green light that seemed to come from a little growth on the walls, like fungus. There was absolutely nothing to see but steps and walls, very neatly cut out of solid rock. It must have been an awful job for those who did all this work, whoever they were.

"Do you think these steps go on for ever and ever?" asked Joe after a time.

"No," replied Gorbo, stopping suddenly. "They've come to an end." He was standing in a little flat place, from which five narrow passages branched out like the fingers of a hand. The question of which passage to take was indeed a hard one.

"We'd better start with the first one," said Gorbo. "Then if it's a wrong one we'll try the next, and so on."

"But suppose we go miles and miles before we find it's a wrong one," objected Joe. "We'd be hours over it, wouldn't we?"

Gorbo scratched his head. " That sounds sound," he observed.

"I know!" cried Joe. "We'll see which one is 'out.' Let Sylvia try. She knows all the out poems."

"All right." Sylvia began to take great interest in the matter now. "Which one shall I try it with?"

"Try the cat one," suggested Joe, after consideration.

So Sylvia pointed her finger at the little tunnels one after the other and repeated:

"If you want to stroke a cat
Lay it flat upon a mat.
Hold it firmly by the tail
Smack it if it starts to wail.
If it starts to spit and shout
Pick it up and throw it OUT."

She stopped with her finger pointing at the fourth tunnel and she looked excitedly at the others, because it was becoming like a game.

"Here we go," said Gorbo, making his way into the fourth tunnel.

They went on and on and on along the tunnel, and just at the exact moment when they agreed that it would never have any end, they fetched up against a blank wall. But on either side was a passage going at right angles, and the question was of course, which was the right one to take?

Sylvia repeated her little mystic rhyme, and "out" was the left-hand turning, so they went along it. After a dozen steps it turned to the right, and a little further on to the left; then it went straight on until it came to an end, with a smooth wall in front and on both sides. There was nothing for it but to go back and take the other turning. They wondered why the people who had done all this work had made this extra blind passage. Joe said they had done it to make it more interesting and adventurous. Sylvia said they had done it because they were pigs. Gorbo said it was merely because they were worse fools than he was and it quite cheered him up.

The other road soon began to turn gently to the left; then without rhyme or reason it turned gently to the right; then to the right and left alternately in very sharp turns. And just when they were convinced that it would go on turning idiotically for ever and ever they came suddenly into what appeared to be a mighty cavern, lighted by the same yellowish-green light of the tunnels, only more so, and full of monster mushrooms.

THE MUSHROOM CAVERN

When I say that the mushrooms were monsters, it hardly gives a correct idea of their size. Under the moderately small ones the three could stand upright, and the large ones were as high as a good-sized cottage and reached nearly to the roof of the cavern. The floor was hard and dry and perfectly flat, and the huge stalks of the mushrooms could be seen like a forest of giant skittles, going into the far distance on all sides. Above, the pink underneaths of those strange specimens showed like an unnecessarily large assortment of giant fancy umbrellas, opened. These, of course, accounted for the cheese-like smell that Gorbo had observed when he first put his head in the little door and sniffed. (It was not exactly like cheese, of course, but cheese is near enough.)

Gorbo showed himself a man of resource in a way. He said that, after all, mushrooms were mushrooms and good breakfast food, and that they might at least have a meal, whatever else happened afterwards. This cheered up Sylvia tremendously and she helped to gather heaps of dried stalks from the floor, and Gorbo got out his flint and steel from his bundle — he rarely went anywhere without his little bundle of tools and other matters and his bow and arrows—and soon had a fire going (to those who may object that mushroom stalks do not burn I have only to say that these did). With the aid of his useful trowel he provided an appetizing series of mushroom steaks, which they all enjoyed tremendously.

They found that the smaller ones were on the whole of a better flavour, and it was while they were searching for some tiny specimens, scarcely as high as a table, in order to cook some more, that they all got a sudden shock. They found that certain mushrooms had large semicircular pieces bitten out of them; the mouth that did it must have been a foot wide, with tremendous teeth. A very disturbing discovery you will say. They looked about them fearfully; and then they heard what sounded like heavy, shuffling footsteps, and a satisfied purring, as of a giant cat.

Gorbo put the children behind him in a hurry and fitted an arrow to his bow (the Snergs bows are on the small size, but they can send an arrow through a two-inch board at close range). Then to their horror appeared an animal that I can only describe as resembling a blonde four-footed walrus walking on its hind legs. It was covered with sleek, ginger-coloured hair, and it had goggling eyes, a mouth that corresponded closely with the estimate they had formed of it from the big bites, and a white drooping moustache. Strange to say, it was a marsupial—that is to say, it had a pouch—but no young ones were peeping out of the pouch as in the case of kangaroos and other marsupials. No, it seemed full of large chunks of mushroom, and the animal was walking upright because it was evidently the only way he could carry them in his pouch without tipping them out. He waddled clumsily up to one of the biggest mushrooms, sniffed at it, purred horribly with delight, bit a large section out of it, and bent his head carefully so as to place it in his pouch. And then Sylvia let out a loud scream.

I do not blame her; perhaps I should have screamed myself if I had been there. But the effect was marvellous. The animal turned its head smartly and stared at them, its fore-paws held up as if in fear and astonishment. The big mouth drooped, giving it a weak appearance; bits of mushroom dribbled from the corners. Then, with a sound like a roaring sob, the animal turned and scuttled away on all fours, scattering sections of mushroom from its pouch as it went.

The sounds of scuttling feet and sobs died away in the far distance and all was silent as before. Gorbo put his arrow back into his quiver. "There's a cowardly custard for you," he remarked, using an expression he had heard from the children. They went back to the fire and had some more breakfast, greatly relieved to find that the denizens of this strange part, so far as they could judge from this sample, were not ferocious ones.

Joe was apparently the bright one: he discovered that there was something like a path going more or less straight through the forest of monstrous fungi, and suggested that it would be a wise idea to follow it. They did so, walking on and on until they were weary of the sight of the thick white stalks, and a good long time afterwards. Strange, is it not, that here Nature should be so lavish of mushrooms, while in England they are so rare that hard-worked men are forced by their wives to rise from their beds before they have had their fill of sleep in order to gather a few poor specimens?

The path came to an end at a blank face of rock. They had reached the other side of the cavern. Sylvia repeated her little poem again, and "out" was to the left, so to the left they went. This time they did not go so very far before they were rewarded by the strange sight of a stone seat, and in front of it, a stone table, both very neatly carved.

What was it doing here? What strange forgotten race had gone to the trouble of chopping a stone seat and table out of hard rock—and not only chopping them out but carving some strange figures on them and smoothing the legs down? They all looked carefully at the carvings; so far as they could judge they were intended to represent rabbits walking upright. Why?

"This cheers me up," said Gorbo. "I can't be the biggest fool. When I consider that people have gone to the length of making this difficult table and bench and carving rabbits on it for the sole purpose—apparently—of eating mushrooms in this dismal cavern, I feel that there is hope for me."

"But we don't think you're a fool, Gorbo," said Sylvia soothingly.

"No, Sylvia," replied Gorbo with a sigh. "But you haven't seen me at my best."

"But there must be some way out close by here!" exclaimed Joe. "Of course they'd put this table near the coming-in place, wouldn't they?"

"You've got it, Joe," said Gorbo. "Unless the people who did it were much worse than me."

Joe was right; at a very little distance away they found a tunnel. It was as narrow as the tunnel they had passed through on the other side and it was just as smooth, but it had this difference, that it sloped upwards, on a gentle slope. They went up it until they were sick and tired of the monotony, and at last they had to sit down, for Sylvia was getting very tired.

When they started off again Gorbo picked up Sylvia in his arms and carried her. "This beastly tunnel's going on like this for about five miles," he said, as he walked on with her. After about twenty steps he put her down again.

"We get fooled every time," he observed bitterly. They had arrived at a little flat place, like a room. Two passages branched out from it, and there was a stone bench on either side, highly finished and each with what appeared to be a pig carved on it.

"Pigs, you see," remarked Gorbo. "However, I suppose they couldn't help it."

Again Sylvia repeated the rhyme and they took the right-hand passage. It went winding about with bold curves for a long distance and then came to a sudden end, but this time, to their great joy, it ended in a small door, iron bound and rusty; like the one they had unfortunately found under the twisted trees. They raised a shout of joy, for surely their long strange journey was over—that is, the underground part of it.

Gorbo pushed at the door, but it did not move. Then he pushed harder. Then he put his shoulder to it and shoved with all his might. And still the door remained shut hard and fast.

"I'll do it!" he cried. "Luckily there's plenty of room for a run." With that, he ran and hurled himself at the door with a mighty crash. And he might as well have flung himself against Westminster Abbey. He sat down and looked mournfully at the children and they looked mournfully back at him.

There seemed nothing for it but to try what the left-hand passage would show them. So they went back and followed it through devious twists and turns until it ended in a small bare chamber, on the walls of which were carved what was undoubtedly meant to represent goats. There was absolutely nothing else to see.

"Goats this time," said Gorbo sourly. "Well, well, well! Yes, it's clear to me that I'm not the worst."

They sat down on the floor and thought melancholy thoughts, for the adventure was beginning to have a very black look. Sylvia hugged the small dog to her, feeling very unhappy. At last Gorbo sprang up and said he was going to have another try at that door if he broke his back at it.

He examined the door all over very carefully. In the sickly greenish light he could see huge iron hinges and plates; certainly it was a very massive type of door for its size. He bent down and put his eye to a tiny chink on one side.

"I can see daylight," he cried excitedly. "We've got to get out! Just watch me this time."

He took a good long run and then came against it with a terrific smash. Then he did it again. After that he did it again. It takes a good deal of bumping to hurt a Snerg, but Sylvia was frightened that he would overdo it.

"Don't, Gorbo!" she cried. "You'll hurt yourself badly."

"I deserve it," said Gorbo. "Yes, I am the worst." He sat down and buried his face in his hands.

"I wonder whether——" began Sylvia. Then she stopped and thought.

"You wonder what?" asked Joe.

"Just an idea of mine. Perhaps—yes I'll try."

She got up and went to the door and grabbed hold of a piece of iron-work where it stuck out a little. Then she pulled as well as she could with her little fingers.

The door opened inwards smoothly and sweetly, and a flood of daylight poured in.

Gorbo looked up, and then smote his head with his clenched fist.

"Never mind," said Sylvia, going up to him and stroking his head tenderly. "Poor old Gorbo!"

THE OTHER SIDE OF THE RIVER

The first glance that Gorbo gave as he came out into the warm sunlight showed him that they were now (as the reader will have guessed from the heading of this piece) on the other side of the river.

This was more serious news to him than to Sylvia or Joe. To them it meant daylight, freedom from the subterranean gloom; possibly the prelude to new adventures (it was). To him it meant trouble and danger and the fear of unknown things. The wide deep river, rushing far below between steep cliffs, had been a barrier keeping the Snergs secure from a horror-haunted land, a land of distressful legends of dragons and other fierce monsters, of Kelps and giants, and a ruthless king who tyrannized over his people. No wonder he gazed sadly at the fair green woods on the other side and wished—chiefly for the sake of the children—that he was less of a fathead.

"It isn't such a nice part on this side," said Sylvia, looking about at a dull landscape, dotted here and there with patches of coarse grass and clumps of thorny trees. "But it's jolly to get out of that dark place."

"Yes, isn't it," agreed Joe contentedly. At his age the present time lasts quite a good bit. "I'm jolly glad we got here. Perhaps we'll have some real adventures now."

"I'm thinking we will," said Gorbo.

They went on a little way and, coming to the top of a gentle slope, saw before them a round grey tower some half-mile or so away. It was surrounded by a high outer wall and looked very lonely and dreary. Gorbo stared long and hard at it.

"Yes," he said at length, "that's old Golithos' tower. I can see him outside, doing something to the wall. I know him by his whiskers."

"Then," said Joe logically, "we'd better scoot. Come along, Sylvia!"

"No, don't scoot," said Gorbo; "it's safe enough. Golithos is quite harmless now because he's reformed. We'd better go over and see if he can tell us how to get back. Don't be frightened, Sylvia, I've heard he's quite kind-hearted now. In fact they say he's rather overdoing it."

Though they were not exactly at their ease (what child is at the thought of visiting an ogre?) they were impressed by Gorbo's confidence, and they went on hand in hand with him towards the tower, Joe carrying the puppy.

GOLITHOS THE OGRE

A huge man, about seven feet high, was working with a heap of mortar and some big stones, repairing a loose part of the wall. As they drew near he turned and saw them; then he smacked his hands together to knock the mortar off and rubbed them in his hair and waited for them with a friendly but weak-looking smile. He had a great silly face and coarse hair and whiskers like bits of a cheap goatskin rug. His dress was the usual shabby dress of ogres in books. It is perhaps slightly unfair to call him an ogre, for as Gorbo had said, he was reformed. Not a child had passed his lips for years, and his diet was now cabbage, turnip-tops, cucumbers, little sour apples and thin stuff like that.

"Aha!" he said as they came up, "you are all heartily welcome. It is long since I had any nice visitors. How are you, my little maid? And you, my little man? And you also, my dear Snerg? Let me see, have I had the pleasure of meeting you before?" He shook hands with them in a very friendly way.

"I don't think so," replied Gorbo. "You see," he added delicately, "I was quite a boy when they—I mean when you—well, when you changed your address."

"Exactly," said Golithos, with a conscious blush. "Well, come inside and make yourselves at home."

There seemed nothing for it but to go on through his door, though all Gorbo wanted was to ask the way back across the river, not to make morning calls. When they were inside Golithos slammed the heavy door and locked it.

"I get so nervous if I leave it open," he explained. "But come in and I'll have a meal ready for you. You must be tired and hungry after your long journey from wherever you have come."

"Look here," said Gorbo, "we don't want to trouble you too much. All we want to know is how to get back across the river."

"To get back across the river," replied Golithos, bending down and placing a hand affectionately on his shoulder, "is easier than you think. Much easier. In fact I think I am right in saying that however easy you think it is it will prove to be easier still."

"Well, I'm glad of that," said Gorbo.

"Naturally you would be. But come inside and make yourselves at home."

"Thanks, but I should really like to know the way."

"The way?" Golithos looked a bit puzzled.

"Yes, the way across the river of course."

"Oh, yes, of course. What am I thinking of? Well, it's perfectly easy. All you have to do is to—but one thing at a time. Come inside and make yourselves at home."

He led the way up some steep steps to a door in the wall of the tower and into a large round room which took the whole of one story. It was big enough, but the most comfortless room possible. At one side was a great four-foot post bedstead, and in the middle was a big heavy table and one big heavy chair. And that was all the furniture, unless you count an accumulation of mixed litter—old clothes and gardening tools and pots and pans and sacks and barrels and so forth scattered on the floor. Some wooden steps led to a trap-door in the ceiling and in the stone floor was another trap-door, with a big iron ring to lift it by, which led apparently to a cellar. There was only one window, with little round panes of dull green glass.

"This is my kitchen-dining room," he said with a look of pride. "I sleep here too—that structure over there is my bed—so it is a bedroom as well. Please take chairs—I mean, one of you take the chair and the others sit on the floor. But whatever you do, make yourselves at home."

"Thanks," said Gorbo. "But what about the way across the river?"

"The river?" Golithos did not seem to grasp his meaning.

"Yes, the river outside. All that wet stuff over there. We want to get back."

"Undoubtedly. Well, you needn't worry about that, because it's a very simple matter. I'll show you how it can be done in the easiest way. But first let's see about dinner." He picked up a pan and a knife and rushed blunderingly down the steps.

"I've heard it said that he's getting very slow since he reformed," said Gorbo after a minute's thinking, "but he's worse than I expected. Somehow or other he makes me feel that I want to contradict him. And I'm not like that usually."

"But he's going to give us something to eat," Joe observed.

"Yes, Joe. But I don't think it will be very strengthening. That's the worst of reformed people. Here he comes."

Golithos came in like a mighty bumble bee, bumping against things and getting his feet entangled with things on the floor and dropping vegetables about and stooping to pick them up and dropping others as he did so. "I'm going to give you the feed of your lives," he said, chopping up lettuce and smiling in his feeble way. "I always think there's nothing so appetizing as fine fresh lettuce and raw onions, especially if they have lots of salt."

DINNER WITH GOLITHOS

In a minute or so he placed a large pan on the table, and then he got two empty barrels and laid a plank across them to make a seat for the children. Sylvia whispered rather anxiously to Gorbo, who had been watching their host with a discontented expression, and indicated that Tiger's contour was losing its curves.

"Look here, Golithos," said Gorbo, "can you give this little dog something to eat?"

Golithos scratched his head. "Let me see—I suppose he doesn't eat salad?"

"No, he doesn't. He's a dog, not a grasshopper. Haven't you got any bread?"

"I may have some odd bits in a sack somewhere. You see I don't eat bread very much. I find its heating to the blood. But I'll try to find some nice bits for him later. In the meantime, let us eat heartily. Would you like the chair or do you prefer standing?"

"Chair for me, thanks," replied Gorbo, seating himself. "Look here, Golithos, this is all very kind and considerate and jolly of you, but these young ones will want something a bit solider than this."

"No solids here," said Golithos quickly. "It wouldn't do."

"Well, you've got a cow outside. Why don't you give them some milk?"

"Milk? Yes, but do you think it would be good for them? It's rather heady stuff."

Gorbo clapped the table smartly. "You hop out and milk that old cow of yours!" he said loudly. "These children want milk. They can't live on lip and lettuce."

Golithos looked fearfully abashed. "Yes, yes, I'll go," he said. "Don't be violent." He blundered out and down the steps.

"Can't quite make him out," said Gorbo. "He was a wicked old rascal once, but if he was rough he was ready—and a bit interesting if you're not too particular. But I think the watercress diet has weakened his brain."

He felt his responsibility in the matter keenly; if he had not been a born fool he would not have got the children into this mess; and his easy-going disposition seemed to have suddenly disappeared with regard to his host. After a minute he jumped out of the big chair and ran to the window and poked his head out. "Golithos!" he called in a warning voice. "Waiting!"

Golithos appeared, bearing a pitcher of milk and looking highly flustered. "Shall I put some water in it?" he asked.

"Give it to me," ordered Gorbo, taking the pitcher. He looked round the littered table and found two earthenware mugs. "Wash them," he said, passing them over his shoulder to Golithos. "Dear, dear, this is barely decent!"

The milk at any rate was nice and warm, and the children felt greatly refreshed by it. A small bowlful was given to Tiger, who lapped it up and then went to sleep on a sack. Then all set to on the salad, Golithos standing by and pressing them to take more whenever they paused. Gorbo took his portion in a dissatisfied way, sometimes looking at a morsel with scorn before putting it into his mouth (I may mention that they were eating with their fingers; there were no forks in this disgusting ménage). After a time he made a crude attempt at polite conversation.

"Doing well here, Golithos?" he asked.

"Pretty well, thank you. Oh, yes. It's lonely, of course; people seem to shun me so. But I have plenty of time to meditate on my past sins."

"Ah, that ought to fill in the time. Keeping pretty fit, Golithos?"

"Tolerably so, thank you. I suffer from stomach trouble occasionally."

"Only occasionally, eh? That's strange. Sleep well, Golithos?"

"Fairly well, I thank you. I have nightmares sometimes."

"What do you expect? This all you're going to give us, Golithos?"

"I'm really afraid I haven't anything else—Yes, I have! I can give you a fine fresh young cucumber."

"Keep it, Golithos." Gorbo stretched himself and yawned and turned to the children. " Well, Sylvia, what do you think of this for a hole? "

Sylvia glanced at the feeble though gigantic face of the once child-eater and felt some pity for him. "Oh, it's very nice," she answered, though not, I am afraid, very truthfully. "Isn't it, Joe?"

"It's fine," said Joe. Then he put his hands before his mouth and spluttered, for his manners were not good. Their host looked very unhappy.

"Just fancy it on a rainy day," went on Gorbo. "Well, Golithos, what's the country like in these parts?"

"I don't know very much about it, because I don't go about very much, but I've heard it's very bad. You see there's the land of King Kul not so very far off, and he's got a very bad character."

"Yes, we've heard of him. What does he do especially?"

"Well, he persecutes the people. You see he makes a hobby of it. And from what I've heard they're the sort of people who ought to be persecuted. But I don't really know much about them because I don't often see any of them. And when I do I lock myself up tight until they've gone. Old Mother Meldrum comes over to see me sometimes and she tells me about the goings-on."

"And who's old Mother Meldrum?"

"Well, she's a witch, that's what she is. She says nothing will go right until King Kul is laid out, and she keeps trying to get me to go for it. But somehow or other I don't feel up to violent exercise since I got reformed."

"You're losing your nerve, Golithos. But why doesn't somebody else try to do him in?"

"I think it's because they're afraid. It's risky, you see. Mother Meldrum says that his castle is three-quarters dungeons. And he keeps six headsmen busy all the time except on Saturday afternoons and Sundays."

"That fits in with what I've heard of him myself," said Gorbo, looking anxiously at Sylvia and Joe, who were taking all this in. "But cheer up, Sylvia, we'll soon get out of it. Now, Golithos, what about how to get across the river?"

GOLITHOS EXPLAINS

The giant took Gorbo by the arm and led him to the window. "Do you see that tree? " he asked, pointing out a tall pine standing far off.

"Yes, Golithos."

"Well, that tree's close by the river, and I pointed it out because it's quite useless your trying to get across the river at that point. Or for the matter of that, at any other point, if you understand me."

"Well, I don't, if you understand me. I can tell you fifty ways how not to get across the river. Rouse your wits, Golithos!"

"You make me nervous. And if you do that you'll drive all the fine ideas out of my head. You see the fact is that you don't get across the river at all. But, notwithstanding, it's a perfectly easy matter to get to the other side if you know the way how. Now do you see my point?"

"I thought I was something of a born fool, Golithos, but since I've met you I'm quite proud of myself."

"Don't speak to me like that; it gives me the all-overs. Look here, all you have to do is to go under the river. You go through a little door."

"I thought so. You've been a long time coming to it, .Golithos. As a matter of fact we came that way, but the little door shut up tight as soon as we got out of it. And there's another door on the other side. How do we get them open?"

"It's quite easy. But I don't quite remember how it's done—now don't get violent! You see it's not exactly difficult; it's only something to do with some little magic spells. You make a circle on the ground and divide it into six parts—or sixteen parts, I forget which. And then you bring some simple little charms-twenty-eight altogether, I think. I know one of them is the toe-nail of the seventh son of a seventh son born on a Friday. And then you repeat something out of a book—oh, if you're going to look at me like that I shall get thoroughly nervous and forget the rest."

"Look here, Golithos," said Gorbo, "do you think Mother Meldrum has more sense than you?"

"Oh, yes, she's got ever so much more! She knows the way to get the door open."

"Oh, does she? Then where can we find her?"

"She may come here at any time. You see she comes because I amuse her—at least that's what she says—and if you wait here a day or two she's bound to turn up. I can give you a lovely room upstairs. I'll move the turnips to one side and give you some nearly clean straw to sleep on. I'd give my own bed to the little ones, but I'm afraid the mattress is rather bumpy; I think some brickbats must have got into it. You see I air the mattress every November, and last November I was doing some building, and as there were a few holes in it, you see—"

"Don't worry, Golithos, we'll take your upstairs room. So come and move the turnips."

THE UPSTAIRS ROOM

The upstairs room was much worse than the one below, which is saying something. It was furnished chiefly with turnips and sacks of lime, and these Golithos began to move to one side in a muddle-headed way, while Gorbo sat on the window-ledge and watched him. At length there was a clear space for the straw, which was spread out in the manner advocated for sick horses.

"There!" said Golithos proudly, resting on his hay-fork, "There's a bed for you!"

Gorbo only snorted and said nothing, and there was silence for a time.

"Those are dear little children," remarked Golithos, trying to be amiable and interesting.

"Yes," said Gorbo shortly.

"It's a long time since I saw any. In my bad old days I saw plenty, as you know, but I thought it best—after I reformed—to keep away from them for a good long time."

"Sound idea."

"Yes, wasn't it? But as I say, these are very dear little things, especially the little girl. Do you know," he went on chattily, "it used to be a saying amongst us in the bad old days that the lighter the hair the tenderer the meat—however, I don't suppose that interests you."

"Not a bit."

"Of course hot. But I have taken quite a strong liking to these little ones. The little girl is very pretty, and they are both well formed. Not fat exactly. I should describe them as well filled out. Chubby, if you understand my meaning."

Gorbo slipped down from the window and went down the ladder in a leisurely way. "Tidy up the place properly," he ordered as he went.

Golithos obediently went on messing about, crooning a little song about a rose that loved a butterfly and faded away.

GORBO'S DOUBTS

It will probably occur to the thoughtful reader at this point that a change had come over the character of Gorbo. A sense of responsibility, mingled with self-reproach, had brought forth qualities hitherto unsuspected, and though he was to some extent losing his natural desire to please all whom he met by conciliatory speech and helpful ways, he was gaining in ability to make quick decisions, as also in verbal fluency and a capacity for what is known among our famed comedians as back-chat.

He found the children in the cabbage patch trying to amuse themselves with Tiger, but not succeeding very well because they were getting very tired of this dismal place. Their surroundings were horrible—all nettles and cheap-looking vegetables and rank grass and stones, and a high wall (on which were lots of snails) shutting out everything but the sky. Sylvia took the puppy to show to the cow, which was the only nice thing in the place and which lived in a rotten old shed in a corner, and Gorbo then had a chance to talk to Joe.

"Joe," he said, "I don't want to frighten Sylvia, but you're a man like me. It seems to me that this is not a healthy place to stay in very long. In the first place we'll get bored to screaming fits, and in the second place I'm having doubts of old Golithos."

"Oo-er!" said Joe, now thoroughly startled.

"Yes, I'm beginning to think he's not so reformed as he thinks he is. Of course it may be only my fancy, but I'm not going to take any risks, and you and Sylvia must keep close by me always. We'll have to stay here a little while because, though it's plain that he won't be able to tell us how to get those little doors open, that old witch may come along at any time, and then I can get it out of her. I'll give her my drinking-horn to tell us how; it's the only thing I've got that's worth anything, but it's got silver on it and perhaps it'll do. But if it's not enough I'm afraid Sylvia will have to give over her little coral necklace. I don't know what witchs' charges are, but I should say the two together would be plenty."

"But won't it be awfully risky staying here?" asked Joe. This was becoming rather more of an adventure than he had bargained for.

"Not so much, because you won't go out of my sight and I've always got my bow tucked under my arm. Of course I could make it quite safe by sending an arrow through his hairy old throat, but somehow I don't quite like to do it until I'm dead certain sure. But don't you worry, Joe. And don't let Sylvia know."

The day wore on. They had a light supper of cold sliced turnips and some of the milk that was left over from the midday feast. They gave a third part of the milk to Tiger in order to moisten some very hard crusts that Golithos found for him. Tiger did not worry, it was quantity he wanted, not quality, and his little abdomen began to take on bold curves again.

GOLITHOS IS TEMPTED

The night passed without trouble. The children slept soundly on their straw; Gorbo had made his bed on top of the trap-door so they felt safe enough. But in the morning there was more than a hint that some good old-fashioned trouble was coming.

Said Golithos to Gorbo (taking him quietly aside by the arm), "Would you oblige me by keeping these dear little children always close by you?"

Said Gorbo to Golithos (removing his arm), "I'm going to. But not particularly to oblige you. What's the little game?"

"It is no little game; it is something more serious. You see I have a horrid fear that I may go back to my old disgraceful ways. The sight of these dear little plump things is a very, very great temptation to me, and I want you to help me to fight against it. I don't want you to go away, because if I don't have the temptation there will be no credit in conquering it—and I really hope and believe that I will be able to. Do you know that last night I wanted to have a look at them asleep, but I couldn't open the trap-door. There seemed to be something heavy on it."

"There was," said Gorbo.

"I thought so. And then, do you know, I came down and sat thinking about them, and after a time I found myself sharpening a big knife in an absent-minded way. It gave me quite a shock. Now promise me that you will help me to overcome this temptation."

"Oh, I'll help you," replied Gorbo.

He called to Sylvia and Joe to come down and to bring Tiger, and then he went with them down the steps to the door in the outer wall.

"Come and open this door, Golithos," he called.

"Oh, you're surely not thinking of leaving me!" exclaimed Golithos, clumping down after them. "I shall be greatly upset if you run away like that."

Gorbo jerked out an arrow and laid it on his bow.

"You'll be more upset in a moment perhaps," he said, "if that door isn't opened before I count ten there'll be three of these sticking out of your silly fat head."

Golithos jumped for the door and had it open just as Gorbo had counted up to six. As the children passed out, shrinking away from him, he bent down and held out his hand to them.

"Good-bye, little dears," he said. "Won't you shake hands with an old reformed person? Oh, this is unkind!"

Gorbo put his arrow back in the quiver and stood for a moment looking up at him. "You stick to watercress," he said tauntingly. "Watercress and cold water. A slice of mangel-wurzel for Christmas. That's about your form."

"You have hurt me," said Golithos, drawing himself to his full height (seven feet, one inch). His tone was not without a certain dignity.

"Get inside!" shouted Gorbo, slipping out an arrow again. "I'm not so sure I shan't——"

But Golithos had scuttled in and banged the door and locked it. They walked along a narrow stony track that led towards some rising ground. Looking back, they saw the head of Golithos peeping over the top of his wall. So far as they could judge at that distance it had a wistful look.

BEYOND THE TOWER

When they had got to the other side of the rising ground and the tower was hidden from view, Gorbo paused in order to take off his cap and tear his hair a little. Then he embraced both children remorsefully, and they gave him such words of comfort as occurred to them.

"The next question," he said, rousing himself, "is the question of what we are to do next. If I knew where Mother Meldrum lived, we'd go straight there at once. But I don't know, and it'd be hopeless my going back to ask Golithos. I've scared what little wits he had clean out of him."

"Perhaps we'll meet somebody if we go on walking." suggested Sylvia. "Then we can ask where she lives."

"Yes, let's," said Joe. "I'd like to meet a witch. We've just had one nice adventure and perhaps we'll have another. Think of it, Sylvia! We are the only two kids in the world who have ever been in an ogre's castle—I mean the only two who have ever got out of it afterwards. Won't the others be jealous!"

"Yes, Joe, but I wish we could go back to them. It's getting too beastly like one of those tales Norah told me."

They walked on and on and on, over a plain which was dotted here and there with clumps of trees but which showed nothing else of interest, until they came to what looked like a road, and this they followed for a couple of hours. Then, suddenly, they saw coming across the plain a man on a horse. The strange thing was that both man and horse were shining all over in the bright morning sun, and they stopped and looked in wonder.

"It's a knight!" Joe exclaimed. "Look, Sylvia! Look at his shining armour and his long lance! I'll bet it's swift and keen." (Miss Watkyns used to sing "I fear no foe" at the Saturday evening concerts.)

"I hope his heart is pure," said Sylvia, rather anxiously. (Miss Ffolijambe used to recite "Sir Galahad.")

Gorbo said nothing, but he tried his bowstring to see if it was all right.

THE KNIGHT-ERRANT

The man in armour pulled up his horse when he reached the road a little way ahead and waited for them. Both children found him rather a disappointment when they came near for he did not seem quite up to the standard of knights in books. It is true that he had shining armour and the lance as long as a barge pole and so forth, but it seemed that his mail suit had not been made to measure. The breastplate was tied on to the back part with what looked like bootlaces, and they did not join well; bits of cloth showed at the sides. The armour on his legs was on the large size and rattled whenever he moved. His helmet also was much too big and it wobbled. The plume, though not a bad plume, should have been smaller to give a good effect. The horse was big and white and hairy, and had a thing like a spiked saucepan lid on its brow.

As they came near he raised the visor of his helmet and stared haughtily at them. From what they could see of his face he had peepy eyes, a long nose and rather puddingy cheeks.

"Who are ye?" he asked in an important way, "and wherefore come ye——" here his voice was cut off suddenly, for the visor had slipped down like a trap and he had to struggle with it.

He got it up at last: "As I was saying, wherefore come ye thus unattended on the King's ways, two children and a dwarf?"

"Who are you calling a dwarf?" said Gorbo disagreeably. "Dwarf yourself!"

The knight gave him a long contemptuous stare in reply, a stare that might have lasted a long time if the visor had not come down again and put an end to it.

"Temper!" said the knight sharply when he had got his visor open. "But we will let it pass. Tell me, have you any wrongs to redress? Sir Percival am I, sworn to succour damsels, to slay giants, wasters, caitiffs and perishers, to rescue——"

"As I was saying," he went on lifting his visor again and propping it up with one hand, "I am sworn to rescue the oppressed, to right wrongs, and to—well, to generally make things happy all round."

"That's very nice of you," said Gorbo. "Then perhaps you'll kindly tell us the way to the witch——"

"Which witch?" interrupted Sir Percival.

"Mother Meldrum. If you'll kindly——"

"Ay, she is known as a parlous witch. She lives in the dark woods where fly the large black bats, all alone with her large black cats, and she gathers herbs o' moonlight nights and brews foul potions to harm honest folk. Which means that I am not going there with you."

"Who asked you to?" said Gorbo. "I only want to know the way there."

"Then in that case you had better travel with me, for I am going within a mile or so of the dark woods. And if anybody should try to oppress you on the way, why, I shall be there to defend you."

"That will be jolly," said Gorbo. "Many thanks. But what about these little ones? Can't you give them a lift—one in front and one behind?"

"H'm!" The knight thought over this for a time. "I'd like to oblige, of course—especially as I am sworn to do good deeds—but wouldn't that make me look rather ridiculous?"

"Not a bit," said Gorbo. "As a matter of fact you'd look rather sweet. Come Sylvia, I'll lift you up."

Before Sir Percival could make any further objection he found that Sylvia had been hoisted up and placed in front of him. The saddle was a roomy one and well padded, so it made quite a comfortable seat for her.

"Catch hold of his belt," said Gorbo. "Then you'll be quite safe. Now then, Joe."

Joe, as a circus-trained boy should, took a run and a flying leap on to the horse's crupper, where he sat at his ease.

"I say," said Sir Percival peevishly, "aren't you rather taking liberties with me?"

"I beg your pardon? " replied Gorbo, who was busy with Sylvia, making a comfortable pair of stirrups for her out of some odd bits of straps on the saddle.

"I said, 'Aren't you rather taking liberties with m?'"

"No, not a bit. Are you quite comfortable, Sylvia?"

"Yes, it's lovely," replied Sylvia.

"And you, Joe?"

"I'm fine. This is a real adventure!"

"I hope this is not incommoding you at all," said Gorbo politely, struck with a sudden idea.

"Oh, no," replied Sir Percival with bitter irony. He couldn't hold his lance properly and he had to reach right round Sylvia to handle the reins. "Who would be incommoded by a little thing like this?" Then his visor fell down again and he roared angrily, though in a muffled way. But Sylvia's handy little fingers soon propped it open again, and she asked Gorbo to find a little bit of stick and sharpen it with his knife. Then she deftly wedged the stick between the visor and the helmet.

"There," she said, patting his steel-cased cheek, "now it will keep up nicely. But what you really need is some large hooks and eyes." She had seen, with the unerring instinct of childhood, that not only was Sir Percival's heart pure but that his head was rather soft.

His perhaps excusable irritation was soothed by this attention, and he smiled at her.

"If any enemies come," she explained, "all you have to do is to pull out this bit of stick and there you are, ready for battle."

Sir Percival was aroused at the mention of battle. "If any caitiffs should oppress you, little golden-haired maid," he said proudly, "I will show you how great a man with his hands is Sir Percival. Evil-doers shake at the mention of my name."

"I don't believe you," said Sylvia, giggling. The child was actually trying on with this belted knight the same ways that had tempted Joe to such flagrant acts of folly and disobedience, and to which their present position might be directly traced. Minx.

" I suppose you can't find room for this little dog?" said Gorbo, holding up Tiger.

"No," replied Sir Percival with stern decision. "I draw the line at little dogs." He then shook the reins and the big white horse started off at a quick comfortable walk.

SIR PERCIVAL'S JOB

Sir Percival seemed to have settled down to inconvenience and (I must own) grotesque appearance due to his having children fore and aft of him on the saddle, and he was quite ready to talk about himself. He was out looking for adventures because he had become enamoured of a young lady, and she had told him that if he would go forth as a knight-errant for one year and conquer a reasonable number of knights and caitiffs and slay some dragons and the like, she would have something to say to him, but she did not say what. So far he had not conquered anybody because he hadn't met anybody who would fight, and as for dragons he really believed they had all left the country. One man, a miller, had told him where there was a dragon, but it turned out that the ribald fellow meant his own wife, who used to go for him with ferocity, and probably with plenty of reason. But he told them he had now great hopes, for he was on his way to a castle he had heard about as being likely—though he didn't know whose it was—for in a castle there were always knights, and knights were always spoiling for a fight. This was very good news to Gorbo because he worked it out that in a castle there was always something to eat, and the children were delighted when he told them this, for the sun was now getting high and they had had nothing to eat since last night's turnips.

In time they came to nice wooded country, which was a pleasant change from the rather bare plain. Then they caught sight of battlemented towers peeping above the tree-tops, and a little later they halted by the outer wall of a small cosy castle, all alone by itself. There seemed to be nobody about, inside or outside, and everything was very peaceful and sunny and still.

THE MYSTERIOUS CASTLE

"I am going to wind this horn," said Sir Percival to Gorbo (he meant, to blow it). "And if you will oblige me by pretending to be my squire, I shall think it very nice of you."

"Yes, I'll be your squire," replied Gorbo, quite interested. He lifted Sylvia down to get her out of the way in case battle should take place suddenly. "I'd like to—Jump down, Joe—I'll tell them you'll take on any six of them and——"

"Not so brisk, please," said the knight. "What I want you to do is to say that I am the famed Sir Percival and—and so on and so forth. Give them the idea that I am something of a terror. Don't know what fear is, and that sort of thing. You see I don't want to injure anybody if it can be avoided, and if any knight prefers to give in without fighting, why, let him do so by all means and save needless bloodshed. Do you get the idea?"

"Yes, I think so. Hot stuff, as it were. Now blow hard."

Sir Percival blew at the small end of the slug-horn and a long melancholy note came out of the other end. Then there was silence for a time; but at length they heard the sound of slow shuffling footsteps coming to the gate.

"Nothing to-day, thank you kindly," said a weak and quavering voice.

"Open, varlet!" cried Sir Percival angrily. "What discourtesy is this to keep a champion waiting at your gate? Open, I say, lest I believe that the knights of this castle fear to meet me."

"Save you, good sir!" replied the quavering voice, "here are no knights, none at all, nor indeed anybody but me and my old dame Margery who look after the castle while the family are away visiting cousins, though we should be glad if they had taken us too for a change of air would do us both good who have been in this same castle until we are sick and tired of the shape of it, to say nothing of the damp which has settled in old Margery's bones so that she goes ever doubled up and——"

"Look here," interrupted Gorbo, putting his hands to his mouth and shouting through the keyhole, "this is the valiant Sir Percival, who has slain so many knights that he has forgotten how many, to say nothing of dragons and such-like. And I am his valiant squire, Gorbo, who is famed for a big appetite, and we have with us two children and a little dog who are also hungry, and the question is whether you are going to be a sport and give us something to eat or whether you are simply going to drive us into smashing up this castle."

"Nay, be not rash, good squire," replied the voice. "I'll open the gate and let you in, for my master hath bidden me give food and drink to wayfarers that need it and especially to those who are liable to damage his stronghold if it be denied them."

The door opened, and to their astonishment there appeared before them, not a doddering old henchman, but a pert young man dressed in the brilliant and fantastic costume of a jester, with one leg of his tights red and the other yellow, and who seemed, from his immoderate laughter, to be having the time of his life.

"Ha, ha!" he cried, joyously, leaping out and slapping Sir Percival on the nose with a bladder tied to the end of a stick. "Did I not befool thee, thou pumpkin face? Even now your jaw is dropped and your eyes goggle with wonder and you have a general resemblance (saving your presence) to a parboiled codfish. Laugh, thou jingling hundredweight of ill-fitting harness"—hitting him again—" and grant this to be a pleasing jest."

SIR PERCIVAL'S ANNOYANCE

SIR PERCIVAL recovered from his astonishment and prepared to do what seemed the only fitting thing to in a case like this. He heaved up his lance to smite this gay young man to the earth.

"For shame!" The young man had dexterously leapt out of the way and crouched down with Sylvia and Joe caught to his bosom. "Would you strike a child?"

"Malapert insect!" said Sir Percival. "Unhand those young ones that I may cudgel you."

"Listen to reason!" bellowed the other, now grovelling on the earth. "This castle is deserted, and I alone know where the larder is. Without my help you will go away an hungered!"

"There is something in that," said Sir Percival, lowering his lance.

"There is a whole lot in it," shouted Gorbo. "Don't hit the poor man!"

The jester bounded up like a tennis ball and flew at Gorbo, enfolding him in his arms. "By this kiss" (kissing him daintily on the top of his head) "I swear eternal friendship."

"Lead on, thou nimble loon," said Sir Percival. "I pardon you if you will take us to the larder without delay."

The jester turned swiftly to the children. "You see yonder door," he said, pointing to a small open door in the main building of the castle, "I'll give you a start of half-way and race you there. Are you ready? Go!"

Sylvia and Joe went off at top speed, and when they were half-way the jester gave a shrill whoop and flew after them, catching up with them just as they reached the door.

THE CASTLE KITCHEN

"This is glorious!" cried the jester, taking a hand of each and leading them into a large comfortable kitchen. Then he turned and looked anxiously at the top of the open door. "No, there's no time to make a booby-trap. Come along and put on aprons."

Sylvia and Joe, both highly delighted with these joyous happenings, were soon dressed in little aprons and caps made out of napkins and busily helping their new friend. He sliced up a ham and got two large frying-pans going, while they put stools round a big table in the middle of the floor and laid plates and mugs and so on.

"Do you think forty eggs will be enough?" asked the young man.

"I think it will be almost more than enough," replied Sylvia, doing a quick sum in her head. "It will be eight each."

"I'll make it fifty then," said the strange being, breaking them thick and fast into the frying-pans.

A heavy clanging sound without indicated that Sir Percival was coming; he and Gorbo had been attending to the horse, supplying it with hay and so forth. As the knight entered the door, the jester turned with an egg poised ready to throw at his head. But he hesitated; then broke it into the pan instead. "I dare not," he said to Joe. "What a pity!"

Gorbo paused as he came in and stood sniffing the delicious smell. He went across to the jester. "Bend low towards me," he said. And when the other had done so Gorbo kissed him on the top of his head. "I also swear a friendship. What are you going to give us to drink."

"I have here," replied the other, making a flying leap over the table to a rough sideboard, "both milk for these little ones and beer for us men. Kindly pledge me," he added, filling up two mugs.

While these two sportsmen were clinking their mugs and gossiping, Sylvia, standing on a stool by the stove, was dripping hot butter on the eggs to give them a choice flavour, and Joe was on another stool pronging out the slices of ham and laying them on a hot dish. They were very happy, because this was a really superior adventure, with food and cheerful things taking place. The castle, too, judging from the kitchen, was a self-respecting place, clean and well kept, and a nice change from the beast of a tower they had spent the night in.

BREAKFAST

Sir Percival was given a stool at one of the tables and Sylvia was put at the other—to serve the food, as she was the only lady present. The ham and eggs were perfect, and they had in addition buttered toast and a pot of damson preserve which the jester said they really must taste as he had made it himself. Tiger had a large plateful of everything and was busily engaged in putting his shape as it should be. (It may be noticed that almost all the news I have to give of this little dog is of the rotundity or otherwise of his stomach.)

"Tell me," said Sir Percival at length, coming to business, "to whom does this castle belong?"

"It belongs to my master," replied the jester. "One Gunthorn, a fierce and rather unscrupulous baron who is something of a scourge to the countryside. I am his privy jester—Baldry is my name—and I ought to know. Many knights have come here, striving to joust with him—but they have all gone, alas!"

"Oh! Where did they go to?"

"Not far, sir knight. There is a graveyard some furlong or so beyond these walls, and there they lie at peace, to each his little headstone. Will you pass your plate for another morsel of ham and some extra egg?"

"No, thank you," answered Sir Percival. "I seem to have lost my appetite. And where is the baron Gunthorn at this moment?"

"Why, sir knight, he may be many, many long leagues from here, and——"

"If I can change my mind," interrupted Sir Percival cheerfully, "I think I could eat another rasher."

"And on the other hand," continued Baldry, passing up the plate, "he may come home at any moment. He went off this morning to look for a wandering knight he had heard about, taking with him his men-at-arms and his cook and household varlets, as is his quaint custom. He left me in charge of his stronghold, knowing that no man dare set foot within these walls, so famed is he for ruthlessness. He has another quaint custom of sneaking in by the postern gate, so that he may observe if all is kept well in his household when he is away. But you do not eat, sir knight."

Sir Percival pushed away his plate and thought deeply. "And what will he do if he finds you entertaining guests during his absence?"

"Good sir," said Baldry earnestly, "I prithee talk of cheerful things while we may. Were he to—but pardon me a moment, did I hear sounds?"

A TERRIBLE MOMENT

He sprang to his feet and stood an instant anxiously listening. Then he bounded over to a door in the corner of the kitchen, flung it open, and disappeared up a spiral stone staircase.

A moment later they heard the distant clanking of mail and a harsh roaring voice raised in anger. The sounds came nearer and nearer and they heard mighty feet descending the stone stairs. Gorbo snatched up his bow and pushed the children towards the door. Sir Percival was struggling to get his helmet on, and making heavy weather of it.

"Good, my lord," they heard the voice of Baldry saying, "if you will but listen to reason――"

"Reason me no reason," interrupted the roaring voice. "If I find unbidden guests in my kitchen I'll first flay them and afterwards slay them――"

The door was flung open and Baldry appeared alone, sweetly smiling and smiting together two pot-lids to imitate the tread of mailed feet.

"Be seated, I pray you," he said with a ringing laugh. "Now was not this a pretty jest?"

"Ay, a right joyous jape," said Sir Percival, pulling his helmet off with violence and displaying a pale and angry face. "Thou art altogether a choice merry varlet. Though how you manage to go on day by day without getting slain passes my understanding."

MORE TROUBLE

"Look!" exclaimed Baldry, suddenly pointing through the open doorway. They could see across the courtyard to the door in the outer wall, and this having been left open showed a perspective of white road leading through the woods. And not so very far along the road horsemen could be seen coming up.

"Now this is no jest at all," continued Baldry, "for here comes the ruthless baron. Let us all go far away and quickly."

"I'm on," said Gorbo, grabbing Sylvia's hand. "But what do you want to go for if you belong to the place?"

"Alas! I never saw or heard of the place before this morning," said Baldry sadly. "I was a-tramping the high road, when by ill-chance I saw that door open and nobody about, and I had just gone in and helped myself to a snack when up comes this valiant knight, thundering at the door and blowing the horn—But all is well!" he cried joyfully, leaping into the air. "He will protect us! Come along, little ones, and let's find a nice spot to see from. Now for the shock of steeds! Now for splintering of lances! Oh, this is heavenly!"

"Well, I don't know so much about that," said Sir Percival disagreeably. He had now managed to get his helmet fixed on and was leading his horse through the door in the outer wall. "You see I don't want to take an unfair advantage of this Gunthorn. He is tired from his journey, belike, and there is no honour in conquering a man who is not fresh and lively. Nay, that were a coward's deed!" He blundered about, trying to mount his horse.

"But, sir knight," pleaded Baldry piteously, throwing himself in front of him, "why spoil the fun? Here is my dear friend Gorbo, who would love to see a jousting. And these little ones, too, see their eager faces! Come, sir, here hangs the horn. One blast and Gunthorn will come spurring up to give you your heart's desire!"

"I know my job better than you," said Sir Percival coldly. "Stand aside, fellow, you will not induce me to take advantage of a weary man—And now you've done it!" he wailed, for Baldry had jumped for the horn and let out a blast that made the echoes ring.

A moment later they saw a man detach himself from the little group of approaching horsemen and speed towards them, handling the longest kind of lance in a manner that bespoke both strength and dexterity. Sir Percival muttered something that sounded like an oath (though I hope it was not) and by a desperate effort managed to get into the saddle. He went in a bumping and jangling gallop in one direction under the trees, and Gorbo and Baldry and Sylvia and Joe and the puppy went swiftly in the opposite direction.

THE SORROWS OF BALDRY

They heard distant shouts, as of annoyed people, which naturally encouraged them to keep up a good speed. Gorbo and Baldry helped the children along with great leaps and bounds, and they were soon deep in the silent woods, far from risk of pursuit. There they rested on a mossy bank and took things easily for a time.

"That was a jolly breakfast, you know," said Baldry, to start the talk well.

"Yes, it was," agreed Gorbo. "But what will this Gunthorn person say when he finds out about your making so free with the place?"

"I don't know. And another strange thing about it is I don't care. And his name's not Gunthorn—at least I don't suppose it is. You see I just made it up suddenly."

"It's quite a good name for a pretence baron," said Sylvia.

"Yes, isn't it?" Baldry was highly pleased at this remark. "It sounds so ruthless. I'm rather good at making up things."

"I'm glad of that," Gorbo said, "because perhaps you can make up some way of getting out of this mess. Do you know the way to get across the river?"

"No, I don't. And I don't know anybody who knows. And I don't know anybody who knows anybody who knows. I wish I did, because I'd like to go with you and see Life. It's very dull in these parts; the people have no sense of humour. And that makes it so difficult for me," he added sadly. "I'm always misunderstood."

"Never mind, poor thing," said Sylvia, who had taken a great liking to him.

"The hollow world," continued Baldry, with a suspicion of tears in his eyes, "believes a jester's job to be all jollity; but little do they think that there may be an aching heart beneath what I must term superficial gaiety."

Sylvia stroked his hand soothingly.

"But on the other hand," he went on in a brighter tone, "there may not be. There isn't in my case at any rate; though I have had a peck of trouble lately. You see, only yesterday I was the King's High Jester, and now I am wandering the earth with only three friends to love me. Four to be exact, because I include this little dog."

"Did you get turned out?" asked Joe.

"No, not exactly; I ran too fast for that. And yet," he went on, with a return to melancholy musing, "it was a quaint conceit, one that might have pleased. Who would have thought that the King was so obtuse. But that is the worst of tyrants, you never, know how they'll take things."

"Tell us about it," said Gorbo, "then you'll feel better."

"Well, it was merely a little idea of mine to brighten up Court life, which has a tendency to become dull and stuffy sometimes. You see it is the King's custom to walk alone through the streets on the day before his birthday so as to show himself to his subjects, and to show that he is willing to unbend from State ceremonial, and so forth. It also serves to brisken their memories with regard to presents."

"What does he do?" asked Sylvia.

"He just walks along, wearing a crown and in his best robes. And he speaks to people here and there—in a dignified way, of course—and he pats children on the head and asks their mothers how old they are, and if they had mumps—and all that sort of thing."

"He seems quite a nice king," Sylvia observed.

"You wait," said Baldry, with dark meaning. "It's only once a year that he bothers about mumps. Well, to go on with my unhappy story, I thought out a scheme for making the whole affair brighter. Though I am young and thin and have no hair to my chin, and though the King is middle-aged and fat and has a flowing beard, I so padded myself up with straw and so painted and behorsehaired myself that when I appeared in the public ways, clad in furred and tinselled robes and wearing a brass crown, there were none that did not take the jester for the king."

"I say, this sounds rather good!" Gorbo exclaimed.

"Oh, it was very good. But listen. In lieu of the customary stately strut of His Majesty, I proceeded in a lively dance, which I have invented myself and which I have named 'The fawn at play' There is in it a great deal of fanciful gesture and nimble leg work. In my right hand I bore a six-hooped pot; my left hand held my robe on high to give free play for my gambols. And thus, with shrill whoops of joy, I pranced among the amazed citizens."

"Did they laugh?" asked Joe.

"Some few of the keener spirits did; but the general expression was of stolid wonder. I redoubled my efforts. Suddenly, on the completion of a series of backward somersaults, I found myself face to face with the King himself. There was that in his countenance that caused me to turn and flee, but I tripped over my robe and fell. In another instant I was seized by the guards and hurried to a dungeon."

"What beasts!" exclaimed Sylvia.

"Yes, Sylvia, that's what they were. And when my gossip, the jailer, told me that the King was frothing at the mouth and had sent for his High Executioner, it seemed to me a choice moment to leave his service if it could be done. My prison was in a tower which had, by great good luck, a drainpipe outside the window, so I washed off all traces of my kingly colour and slipped down. I reached the ground without other mishap than a rasping of my knees and knuckles and fled afar. Better to roam the cold world than to await the vengeance of a tyrant. So here I am, alone with you dear things in the greenwood. And very nice too."

"Is the King very ruthless?" asked Sylvia anxiously.

"Ruthless! Oh, my! However, I'm not going to go into details because that would only frighten you and serve no useful purpose."

"We've heard that things are pretty bad on this side," said Gorbo. "And Golithos said the same."

"Oh, yes, dear old Golithos. You told me you'd stayed a night with him. I've never seen him myself, but I thought of paying him a visit."

"Don't you do it," said Gorbo. "He'll bore you stiff—and there's nothing to eat at his place but the stuff rabbits eat."

"Then that settles that," said Baldry. "Well, where shall we go?"

"We'd better try to find Mother Meldrum somehow. She'll be able to tell us how to get back home."

"Dear old Mother Meldrum!" exclaimed Baldry. "Yes, let's go and find her; she lives somewhere in the dark woods, which are somewhere about here. I've always wanted to meet that dear old lady, and now I shall!"

"Is she nice then?" asked Sylvia, rather relieved at his enthusiasm.

"Well, I wouldn't go as far as that. She's a witch, and she's rather noted for blighting crops and injuring folks generally and she makes a fairly good living by selling curses and nobody of any sense will go near her. But she may have her good points. Let's go at once!"

"Look here, my dear friend," said Gorbo, "this is all very well for you and me, but what about Sylvia and Joe? You stay here and look after them and I'll go and see her. There's no need for all of us to come."

"No, Gorbo," cried Sylvia, "we're going where you go."

"Of course we are," said Joe. "Besides, it'd be rather fun to meet a real witch."

"That's my way of looking at it," said Baldry. "Fun is the correct word. Come along, Joe, let's look for the dark woods. I'll race you to the top of that tree."

He ran to an enormous tree a little distance away and Joe ran after him. In another minute the two disappeared among the leaves. Then cries of joy were heard from aloft.

"It's lovely up here," called Joe. "Swinging about like Billy O!"

"And the dark woods!" called Baldry. "Miles and miles and miles and miles of dark woods. Oh, this makes life really worth living!" (Certainly he seemed the kind that is easily pleased.) "Come down, Joe, we'll show them the way."

The two came scrambling down, and they all went on and on until the trees came to an end at a wide stretch of turf that sloped gently away before them. And about half a mile or so away there were other woods, stretching as far as they could see on either hand.

Undoubtedly the dark woods, for nothing in the shape of woods could be darker or more dismal looking.

THE DARK WOODS

They went on and soon reached the edge of the sombre trees on the opposite side, and then the question was, of course, which way were they to go. Gorbo was of opinion that they had better go as straight as they could and keep their eyes open for anything like a witch's house, but Baldry suggested that they should sit down comfortably and shout for Mother Meldrum at intervals and see if she would turn up. And considering the vast extent of the dark woods both proposals seem to me ridiculous.

The question was settled for them by the sudden appearance of a man who came walking out from the wood. He was dressed in a woollen jerkin and hose and instead of a hat he had a hood with a cape to it, as in the pictures of the cheaper sorts of mediæval people, and he carried in his hand a little packet done up in leaves. From the expression of his face they judged he was not a nice man. He stared at them for an instant and then spoke angrily:

"Oh, yes, a man can't buy a little curse without a lot of busybodies following him about! I'm not going to use it on you, am I?"

"We hope better things of you, sweet chuck," replied Baldry. "All we want is the way to Mother Meldrum's place."

"Oh, then all you have to do is to follow this little path." The man appeared to be greatly relieved. "But she's out of curses; I got the last one. You see there's been rather a run on them lately."

"We've only come for a couple of blessings," said Baldry, as he took Sylvia's hand and ran along the little path, followed by the others. They heard the man shouting that in that case they were going to the wrong shop, but they did not stop to argue the matter, and in a few minutes they found themselves deep in the shadow of tall mournful trees that shut out all but little chance glimpses of the sky. On either hand they could see patches of black swampy water, but the track was fairly plain (giving a hint that Mother Meldrum did a brisk business) and they went along at a good rate. There were no birds or cheerful little animals in this horrid place, but there were—as they soon became aware—bats.

Compared to these the bats of the twisted trees were little pets. These measured six feet or more across the wings and they had beaks of enormous size, from which issued hoarse bubbling sounds. Sylvia, who liked bats as much as she liked black-beetles, pulled her napkin cap over her eyes (she still wore this little stolen head-dress) and shuddered; but it was too late to think of turning back now however much she would have liked to. She kept close under Gorbo's arm, and in time she began to be more used to them; after all they only flopped about and bubbled, and did not bite, which is the main thing.

At length, late in the afternoon, after a journey that was very tiring to the young ones, they came to a part where the forest seemed a little clearer and lighter and not so swampy. The track went on for another half-hour's travel and then they saw before them a house which they knew must be Mother Meldrum's, if only because nobody but a witch would select it for a home.

MOTHER MELDRUM'S HOUSE

There was a little shabby patch of grass in front of the house, but behind and at the sides it was closely surrounded by trees and thick bushes. It seemed to be mostly roof—an untidy roof of thatch that reached nearly to the ground in some places and twisted up into gables here and there over ugly little windows like eyes. Although it was by no means a big house it looked somehow as if it had rather a lot of little lopsided secret rooms, and it had what I may call a generally wicked appearance. One could not imagine kind silver-haired people living in it and doing good deeds to the poor. It had its effect on Sylvia, who hung back a little as they came near; and even Joe showed no anxiety to get inside.

"I think we'd better tie Tiger up in one of these napkins," said Sylvia. "You see Sir Percival said she had black cats, and if Tiger takes to chasing them about she may get angry."

"Yes, Sylvia," said Gorbo. "That's a good idea. We must keep her in a good temper."

So the puppy was tied up carefully in a napkin, with only his nose out, and carried in Sylvia's arms. Then Baldry—who suggested that he should be the spokesman because of his ready wit—rapped smartly at the door.

"Who knocks?" called a disagreeable voice.

"I, good mother, Baldry the King's High Jester. And I have with me my dear old friend Gorbo and my dear little friends, Sylvia and Joe, to say nothing of their small hound. And we have come a long, long way to pay our respects to you."

"Pull the string of the latch and come in," said the voice.

Baldry did as he was told and they all went into a fairly large low-ceilinged room which looked like a kitchen. At the chimney-place a tall old woman was standing, stirring up a pot. She turned and looked at them, and Sylvia gave a little squawk at the sight of her face, which was indeed horrible.

"Here we are again!" cried Baldry, cutting a swift caper and then striking an attitude calculated to put anybody into a good humour.

"What do you mean by 'again'?" asked the old woman with a scowl. "You've never been here before."

"Well, good dame, it means—well, it means 'Here we are and let's be jolly' or words to that effect. It's an expression in common use among jesters," he added lamely, for the old woman merely turned round and went on stirring the pot.

"So that's what it means." She tasted a spoonful of soup from the pot in a leisurely way. "I see. And does the King laugh when you say that?"

"Yes—sometimes."

"Ah!" she said, "I've heard he's not quite in his right mind."

Now this was an unsatisfactory reception, and they all four felt very uncomfortable standing in the middle of the kitchen, with the old woman's back turned to them as she went on stirring. The room was very dark, for there was only one small window at one end, shaded with thatch, and there was not too much light outside owing to the trees. But every now and then the fire would flicker up and give them glimpses of articles such as a witch would be likely to have about her—bundles of herbs that looked poisonous and a stuffed alligator hanging from the rafters, and so forth. Poor Sylvia need not have worried about Tiger chasing the witch's cats, for things were the other way about. Six or seven of the biggest and blackest cats that ever lashed a tail came crawling out of corners and rubbing themselves against her so that she could hardly keep her feet, all the while purring like horrible snores, their green eyes fixed on the napkin that held the shivering Tiger.

After a couple of minutes or so the old woman turned round and seated herself on a stool and looked at them. "Are you the one who squealed just now?" she asked Sylvia.

"Ye—yes, Mrs Meldrum," replied Sylvia faintly.

"You'd better not do it again. Now then, one of you! What do you want?"

"We only want to know how to get back across the river, please, Mum," said Gorbo politely.

"Ah, you're a Snerg, I see. How did you get here?"

Gorbo gave her a brief account of the result of his fatheadedness, and Mother Meldrum chuckled.

"What will you give me if I tell you?" she asked after a while.

Gorbo brought out his silver-tipped horn and laid it on the table. "If this little christening present will do, Mum——"

"What else?"

"I'm afraid I haven't anything else really valuable, Mum. But Sylvia here has a little coral necklace——"

"Let's see your necklace, Sylvia," said Mother Meldrum.

Sylvia took it off and gave it to Gorbo, who handed it to the old woman. She glanced contemptuously at it and threw it on the table.

"What else?"

"That's all we've got, Mum—except clothes."

She looked at the clothes of all of them in a general way. Then she reached out her arm and fingered the material of Sylvia's frock. Then she sniffed.

"This little lot," she said, nodding at the horn and necklace, "will just about pay a tenth part of what I want to show you the way."

There was an unpleasant silence for a time. Even Baldry appeared to have mislaid his blithe disposition. Though he had expressed a desire to meet the witch, now that he had the opportunity he did not seem to enjoy it. The truth is he was overwhelmed by what is known as the personality of the old lady.

"Make me laugh," she said, suddenly turning to him.

MORE SORROW FOR BALDLY

"Er—laugh, good mother?" he replied. "Oh, yes, of course. Would you like———"

"I want to be amused," she interrupted angrily rapping on the table. "It's your job, isn't it? Don't stand there like a pump but say amusing things!"

"I'll do my best, dame," said Baldry, rousing himself. "Perhaps a few rib-tickling conundrums will please you. If so, tell me the difference between an unripe gooseberry———"

"Shan't!" shouted Mother Meldrum.

"Oh—then would you like a merry song?"

"Not a bit."

"Oh—then perhaps—perhaps a jolly tale would please you."

"Let's hear your jolly tale," she said, after a moment's consideration.

"Well, then, good dame," said Baldry, making a special effort, "there was once an honest collector of the King's taxes who———"

"Don't believe it."

"But this one was honest," pleaded Baldry.

"Then why didn't you say he was a freak? Go on."

"And this collector of taxes was on his way home after the day's toil, riding on his ass, when he met three beggars, who begged of him———"

"Well, that's what they usually do, isn't it? What's there funny about that?"

"Nothing very much," replied Baldry. "But it will get better as I go on."

"Go on, then, what are you waiting for?"

"And so, good dame, being charitable as well as honest, he gave to the first beggar a penny, to the second a piece of sausage, and to the third a small loaf of bread. But the first beggar, having had a full meal some half-hour before——"

"Excuse me for stopping you," interrupted Mother Meldrum, "but I don't think I care to hear any more. You say it is meant to be a funny tale, don't you?"

"It is generally so considered," replied Baldry sulkily.

"To me," said the old woman, "it's about as funny as a bilious attack."

To those who know from experience—as I confess I do—how painful it is to have one's verbal efforts to be sparkling received with cold, unappreciative looks or smiles in which pity lurks behind a mere pretence at mirth, will appreciate how Baldry suffered from this really pointed rudeness. He stood looking miserably at the venomous old person, too distressed to notice that Sylvia was endeavouring to console him by patting his hand. His profession was to make laughter, to spread good humour, to (at meal times) set the table in a roar; yet he was roaming the earth, an outcast, because of the ill-success of his late jest with the King, and now he had failed again. Was he losing his power to captivate? That is what troubled him.

A CHANGE OF TONE

Mother Meldrum got up and went back to her cooking, leaving them standing, with Sylvia still knee deep in black cats.

"Look here, Mum," said Gorbo, after an uncomfortable interval of silence, "Golithos told me you'd be kind enough to tell me——"

"Golithos?" The old woman turned round smartly. "So you saw Golithos, did you?"

"Yes, Mum, we stayed one night at his place. He said you came to see him sometimes, and he told us to wait there for you."

"Then what made you leave him?"

"Because—well, because——." Gorbo felt that perhaps, if she was friendly to Golithos, she might not think highly of his offer to send three arrows through his head.

Mother Meldrum went to her stool and sat thinking and thinking, with her eyes wandering from Gorbo to the children. Suddenly she gave a tremendous chuckle that made them all jump. Then she jumped up briskly and patted Sylvia on the shoulder and told her to sit down.

"And sit down, all of you," she went on. "What are you all standing for? There are stools enough. You must be hungry too, but I'll soon have some dinner ready. I wouldn't like you to go away saying that old Mother Meldrum didn't feed you properly."

Though they did not understand this very decided change of manner (who would?) it was very welcome. Gorbo put his bundle and his bow and arrows in a corner, and got a basin of water for the children to wash in. Then he washed his own piece of comb and gave it to

Sylvia to put her hair in order, and when she had done this Joe had a turn at the comb. Tiger was put by Mother Meldrum's advice in a little coarse basket and hung up on a hook in the ceiling, and there he sat moaning a little while the fierce black cats roamed to and fro and looked up at him with shining green eyes and sniffed as if he smelt good to them.

DINNER WITH A WITCH

In a little while Mother Meldrum began to slap platters on the table, and into each platter she put two large ladle-fulls of stewed hare, with potatoes, carrots, peas and onions, which had a most delicious smell, and told them to pitch in. A flask of wine—of a rather harsh flavour but not bad—was placed on the table for the grown-ups, and the children were given a little taste in water. Mother Meldrum was now quite kind and considerate: when Joe spilled a lot of his stew on the table she said it didn't matter, that these things would happen. Baldry plucked up his spirits with the good food and drink and the agreeable change of manner, and told a couple of short tales which were well received by all present, Mother Meldrum being especially tickled.

When dinner was over the bits were given to the cats, who gnawed and growled like lions, and to Tiger, who had his ration aloft in the basket. The children offered to help by washing up, and they and Baldry were soon busy outside with a small tub of water and some kitchen cloths, putting a polish on the plates and things.

"And now let's talk," said Mother Meldrum to Gorbo, "You want to get back across the river. Very well, I'll settle it for you. What's more I'll only charge you that horn and that measly little necklace for doing it."

"Oh, thank you, Mum!" cried Gorbo gratefully.

"I always like to help when I can. But before I can do it you'll have to give me a hand. I'm clean out of mandrakes, and I'll need six or eight to work the spell, so you'll have to go and get me some to-night, because you can only get them when the moon's shining. The place is about a couple of miles from here."

"I'll bring you back a barrow load of them," said Gorbo, who did not know what they were. "Just show me the place and——"

"Not so fast," said the old woman snappishly. "Mandrakes don't grow like bluebells. You'll likely have to spend all the night looking for them. You see they're little roots shaped like persons, but there's the true mandrake and the spurious mandrake. There's about ten thousand of the real ones to one of the others."

"Oh! Then how do I tell the difference, Mum?" asked Gorbo.

"When you pull them up. The real ones squeak."

"Oh!" Gorbo did not relish the idea of a night alone in the moonlight in these distressful woods, pulling up things that squeaked. But there was no way out of it. "Very well, Mum," he said. "And what shall I do with Sylvia and Joe?"

"They can stay here with me. The funny man can stay too and look after them. Your job is to come back in the morning with at least six nice lively mandrakes. It's rather a swampy place where they grow, but you won't mind that. If any things come and look at you don't be worried, but don't speak if you can help it because it's best not to."

"What sort of things?" asked Gorbo.

"Well, mostly things rather like people, only with big ears and slobbering mouths. Oh, and take a stick with you on account of the bats. As a rule they're harmless, but they've been known to bite when you're not looking—stooping and so forth. As it's getting on to night you'd better get ready to go now, so here's a basket. I'll go with you and show you the place."

Gorbo shivered and took the basket, but he did not look enthusiastic.

"None of your sulky looks!" cried the old woman with sudden fury. "Just put on those airs and I won't do a thing for you!"

"I didn't mean to be sulky, Mum," said Gorbo. "I'll go at once. You'll—you'll look after the little ones, won't you?" The poor chap felt very doubtful about leaving them for the night; Baldry and he had sworn a friendship, but he did not have much belief in his power to protect them. But there really seemed no way out of it.

"That's better," said Mother Meldrum. "Yes, I'll look after them very nicely. You come with me and I'll show you where they are to sleep; then you'll feel easy in your mind."

THE SPARE BEDROOM

She called the others and then took a candle and went to a door in the darkest corner of the kitchen, which led to a flight of narrow stairs, and then to a dark passage above. There were two or three little closed doors on either side of the passage, but there were no windows anywhere and they had to be careful how they walked, for the floor was very uneven and at one place there were two steps up and at another three steps down. At the end it turned round a corner, and there was another door which led to another narrow flight of stairs and up to a big room, full of what seemed to be bundles of herbs hanging from the rafters, and with only one tiny window high up near the roof. She went quickly over to a door at one end of the room and slammed and locked it, as if there was something inside that she didn't want to come out, then she took them to another door at the other end and told them to come in.

They found themselves in a little room, dark like every other part of this horrible house, as it had only a small window half hidden by creepers, and thatch. There was absolutely no furniture in it but a four-post bedstead, and a little pair of steps to use when going to bed, so high was it from the floor. From the window they could see only the gloomy tree-tops fading away in the dusk that was coming on, and a glimpse of the moon peeping out from a stormy cloud.

Sylvia stood with Tiger in one arm and held tightly to Gorbo. Baldry was doubtfully swinging his bladder stick which with the exception of his clothes was his only possession. Nobody looked cheerful except old Mother Meldrum, who was quite brisk.

"Now you dear little things can go to bed at once," she said. "There's enough moonlight for you to see by. This funny man can have a bed in the kitchen and the Snerg will come with me for a little walk."

"Are you going to leave us alone, Gorbo?" asked Sylvia in a whisper.

"Yes, Sylvia," he replied, putting his arms round her, " but I'll be back early in the morning. You see I've got to go and help Mother Meldrum get some things she wants to help us get across the river and back home, so you do as she says and go to sleep."

"Oh, come along with you!" cried Mother Meldrum impatiently. "I can't stay here all night. Tumble into bed, both of you!"

It really seemed that there was nothing else to do. Sylvia took off her slinkers and then looked round to see if there was anything in the shape of a nightie; but there wasn't, and the old woman let out such a snarl at the delay that both children bolted into bed, all standing, as sailors say. Gorbo tucked them up with a patchwork quilt and kissed them both very sorrowfully and put the puppy at the foot of the bed; then he went out after the others.

"There's your bed," said Mother Meldrum to Baldry, pointing to a large box with straw in it in the corner of the kitchen. "Curl up and go to sleep. Dream of some funny things for to-morrow."

"It's full of cats," said Baldry discontentedly, as he looked into the box.

"Heave them out then, you helpless loon!" shouted Mother Meldrum.

Baldry sighed deeply and began removing cats. They all growled and spat at him, and one bit him finely in the fleshy part of the thumb. Gorbo whispered to him to keep a good look out for the children, and then picked up his bow and basket and so forth and went out after the old woman.

WHAT HAPPENED IN THE NIGHT

Strange to say, the children dropped off to sleep almost at once. They were tired with the long walk and the bed was fairly comfortable, and Joe, who, as I have said, was always the true optimist, had comforted Sylvia by cheering remarks about everything coming out all right even if it was a beast of a house.

Joe woke out of a sound sleep with a start. It seemed to him that he had heard a loud crack somewhere. He sat up and looked about him, wondering where he was. Then he remembered the shape of the little window, through which the moonlight was now streaming brightly, just touching Sylvia's curls as she slept peacefully beside him with the puppy curled up in a ball behind her neck. He lay down again, and was just dropping off again into a delicious sleep when he heard another crack, and this time he was out of bed with a jump, for there was a dark shadow at the window and the lattice was wide open.

"Joe!" called a whisper, "it's me, poor old Baldry. Don't make a sound."

"What's wrong," whispered Joe, creeping to the window.

"Everything. Wake up Sylvia and tell her to come quietly." Baldry was climbing carefully through the window. "We've got to get away quickly."

Joe was a sensible boy (in some ways) and he wasted no time in questions but shook Sylvia carefully and then put his hand over her mouth and whispered to her not to speak. She rubbed her eyes and stared at Baldry. Then she became fully awake.

"Yes, Joe," she said, not trembling very much, "I'll be a sport." She jumped out of bed and put on her slinkers (there were the elements of greatness as well of flirtatiousness in that child). Baldry put his arms about them so that he could whisper what he had to say.

"There's a man that's come in with Mother Meldrum—a giant—and they're down below talking. And I'm pretty sure it's Golithos."

"Oo—er!" said Joe with a jump.

"Yes, it's a great big man with lots of hair and whiskers and a great silly face, just as you told me. They came in through a back door somewhere, so that they wouldn't wake me I suppose, and they sat talking and talking in a back room. So I crept up and looked through a little chink and I saw him quite plain, Joe. Horrid sight. And she got furious with him and called him a cowardly lubber and said if he didn't do it he shouldn't have a single bite at them."

"What did she mean?" asked Joe.

"Well, I don't know what she wanted him to do. But about the biting, Joe, I think she meant you and Sylvia."

"Let's scoot!" said Joe.

In a minute or two they had the sheets torn into long strips and knotted together, and Sylvia was tied with this handy rope under the arms and lowered gently out of the window, holding Tiger tightly to her. Joe in the meantime was going down by way of a big creeper that grew against the wall, and by which Baldry had climbed up to them. As soon as he was on the ground Baldry's red and yellow legs shot out of the window, and in another minute he was down beside them.

"Come along," he said, grabbing a hand of each one, and running with them into the trees, "there's enough moonlight to find the path, I think. But in any case we've got to get somewhere else quick."

"But what about Gorbo?" asked Joe, stopping suddenly. "What'll he say when he finds we're gone?"

"Yes, we can't leave Gorbo behind," cried Sylvia. "Oh, what are we to do?"

"We've got to go," said Baldry. "Golithos has come after you, that's plain. And I'm afraid I'm not much use in a fight; I've only got my little bladder stick. But Gorbo's a hard little man with lots of fight in him, and he's got his bow and arrows. He'll be able to look after himself all right, and when he finds we're gone he'll chase after us, you can be sure of that. We'll go on and hide just outside these beastly woods and wait for him to come."

This seemed reasonable enough, and they started off again at a run. But though the moonlight was bright enough when it shone on the path there were long stretches where it was quite dark, and Baldry had often to walk ahead of the children and feel the way. They moved on slowly, sometimes running a bit but more often crawling along, always with the thought that they might at any moment hear that dreadful couple coming after them and shouting to them to stop; and it shows what a plucky girl Sylvia was that she could keep up without a murmur, even though her little heart was heavy with fear.

At last they found the moonlight giving place to the grey light of dawn, and they were filled with joy and thankfulness, for things that are terrible in the night seem almost harmless when the day comes. And, feeble though the light was yet, it enabled them to pick the path much more easily: however bright the moon shines it casts black shadows, but the light of day gets behind things.

"Do you think they will come after us?" asked Joe. With the little bit of light and the extra speed they were making he felt that the subject was at least bearable.

"No," replied Baldry, "not yet awhile I think. Old Mother Meldrum's too busy jawing and Golithos is too busy eating."

"What is he eating?" asked Joe, struck with a sudden idea. "Salad?"

"No, Joe, he'd got a lot of big beef bones in his bag and he was biting hard at them while he listened to that old beast."

"Oh, he's killed that nice cow!" cried Sylvia. And though she had borne all the terrors so bravely she burst out crying at the fate of the patient animal that had been so friendly to them and given them milk in their sore need.

THE GREEN RIDE

When at last they came to the end of the dark woods the sun was over the tree-tops and everything looked delightfully bright and cheering. They raced across the wide stretch of turf that separated them from the nice friendly-looking forest on the other side, and they were soon resting in a warm spot just at the outskirts of some spreading oaks, far from the horrible house and the haunted woods.

Baldry said it was best to stay exactly where they were and keep a good look out for Gorbo, who would certainly chase after them as soon as he came back and found they were gone. Of course if Golithos or the old hag came out first it would be necessary to hide closer, and he looked round and found a nice place, deep in a thicket of bracken, where fifty people could be safely hidden, and to which they could do a bolt at a moment's notice.

But now that they had their minds at rest to some degree, the conversation turned on things to eat and drink; there is nothing like exercise and fright to give one an appetite. Sylvia said how nice it would be to have a hot cup of tea with plenty of milk, and Baldry, who belonged to mediæval times and therefore did not know of tea, asked if it was anything like hot spiced ale. This led the talk to hot ham, to eggs cooked in various ways, and buttered toast. And the result was they got ravenous.

Baldry was knitting his brow over the question of how to get breakfast when suddenly they heard clanging sounds and the clump of horses' feet. And looking about them they saw a cavalcade of some ten or twelve men-at-arms, coming along the green ride with much pomp and glittering of steel and high stepping of fine horses. Baldry stared earnestly at them and then he gave a satisfied chortle.

"These blokes," he said (blokes is not the word he used of course, but it is the nearest I can get to it in translation), "are the same ones who rode up to the castle yesterday and frightened dear Percy away. But they didn't see us, because we got away so quickly, so I think we had better see if they can spare us a trifle. Men-at-arms generally have some bits of food about their persons—cold fried fish and sausage and the like—and they're generally good-natured on a fine morning. And if they give us some little pieces of money instead we can buy some breakfast somewhere—If there's a house anywhere in these wild parts."

"All right," said Joe, starting up. "Come along, Sylvia."

"No, wait a bit," said Baldry, "this wants thinking out. To make this thing a success we have to appeal to them in some quaint way. I've got it! You go first, Joe, turning somersaults; that will make them stop and wonder. Then you go next, Sylvia, and drop a nice little curtsey and smile at them; that will put them in a good humour. Then I'll come along walking on my hands, and that will make it a sure thing and they should unbelt at once. First of all let's make ourselves look nice."

The children were highly interested and Sylvia asked him if he had a comb. But he had not, so she fluffed out her curls with her fingers and then knelt over a little forest pool close by to make sure that she looked rather fetching. (She was her mother's daughter all right enough.) Joe tucked his shirt in neatly and tightened his belt, and Baldry practised an expression of attractive mirth.

The horsemen approached at an easy walk and they could see the face of the leader, an able-looking person whose well-fitting and polished mail and golden spurs proclaimed him a knight in a prosperous line of business. He rode with his visor raised, talking to one whose plain steel spurs and armour devoid of fancy trimmings showed that he was as yet but a squire. In the still morning air their voices came clearly to the little waiting group.

"In sooth, good Baldwin," he was saying, "there is now little chance of honourable adventure in the land. But yester morn I had hope of running a course with the scurril Sir Percival, who has dared to raise his lobster eyes to my mistress and to brag forsooth that she has sent him forth seeking advancement to grace her name. But the pestilent knave fled and my hope was dashed to the ground—which is a pity, because that's what I meant to do to him."

"Good, my lord," said the squire, "'tis likely that the Lady Gwendoline did but tell him to chase himself. So at least went the gossip at the buttery hatch."

"My lady has a pretty wit, and perchance she put her answer in such wise that the moth-eaten rascal has construed it to his own undoing—or at least to his grievous waste of time. But what mummery have we here, good Baldwin?"

It was Joe, turning brisk somersaults, and the leader halted his horse and stared down at him. Joe sprang at him and clasped his mailed leg with his arms, as Baldry had told him to, and loudly asked for charity.

"Unhand my left leg, thou wanton!" cried the leader. "Who told you to behave like this?—But whom else have we here?"

This was Sylvia, who came tripping up and dropped a dainty curtsey, smiling very prettily at him.

"By my hilt, a right winsome little lass! Is she not, Baldwin?"

"Ay, my lord, she has hair like ripe corn and merry blue eyes, and her cheeks are like rose leaves in the morn. A pretty maid—and a saucy, I warrant me."

"You silly thing!" said Sylvia, pretending to be coy; "I don't believe you." (This sort of behaviour came quite naturally to her.)

"Nay, little lass," said the leader, smiling good-humouredly, "for the sake of your pretty looks I have here a silver groat"—he pulled off his mailed glove and fished about in a little steel pocket in his cuisses, or thigh armour—a quaint little pocket that shut with a spring. "I know I had a groat somewhere—Ah, here we have it!" He bent down and placed the coin in Sylvia's little palm and patted her cheek. "And if you are hungered my good squire has half a fat capon which he borrowed—But whom else have we here?"

Whom else they had was of course Baldry, who came along, walking upside-down and singing "When woods are green and foules sing," a truly difficult feat before breakfast you will say. When opposite the knight he sprang right side up and cut a dexterous caper—and then stared in horror.

"Scurril rogue!" roared the knight, catching him by the collar with a grip of iron. "At last we have thee who dared to put so scandalous a jest upon His Majesty! Ho, there, seize me this knave and loose him not till he be safe in the royal dungeon."

CAPTIVES

Words cannot describe the dismay and mental confusion of Joe and Sylvia at this unhappy change of fortune, or I should certainly try for it. Their pleadings that Baldry be allowed to remain with them met with no satisfactory response from the leader, and when they exclaimed against his conduct in taking away their companion and protector and leaving them alone in the forest, he merely stated that all this talk was unnecessary for they were coming along too. I will pass briefly over their indignation at this new tyranny; of how Joe in the first flush of his wrath called the knight "Blighter!" or how Sylvia stroked his mail-clad hand and implored him not to be a beast. Suffice it to say that all was of no avail and that they were lifted up and placed each in front of a stalwart man-at-arms, while Baldry was ordered to mount a spare horse they had with them.

Strange to say, now that Baldry was captured and there was no way out of it, he took the matter with more philosophy than might be expected. He climbed up on the horse as he was told, loudly calling all to witness that he was doing so under protest, and seated himself facing the tail; and when the squire, Baldwin, sternly reproved him for his folly he apologized in such ironical terms that the men-at-arms were forced to turn away their heads to hide a smile. Encouraged by this he broke loudly into song, but here the knight took a hand in the matter and ordered them to tie his mouth up with a kerchief. Then he placed himself at the head of his men, gave an order, and the troop turned round and went back over the green ride.

Truly a bitter result of the children's folly and disobedience to find themselves borne far from their faithful friend Gorbo, to become the captives of a king of ruthless fame.

And as the troop rode on, two and two, old Mother Meldrum was standing, out of breath, at the edge of the dark wood, glaring at them from under her hand and muttering deep curses.

PART III

THE DOINGS AT HOME

It will be well at this point of the narrative to return to the land of the Snergs and consider the doings of King Merse II and his friend Vanderdecken.

During their conference they had come to the decision that the children and Gorbo must have got by some strange chance to the other side of the river and were wandering about in the unknown country beyond, where not even a Snerg had penetrated, or, for the matter of that, ever wished to penetrate. There was nothing for it, therefore, but to devise some means of following them there in force and rescuing them; though from what dangers they were to be rescued no man could say.

Vanderdecken had considered carefully and asked whether, as the river must reach the sea at some point, they could go along the coast and cross it at its mouth. But King Merse told him that not only was it very far to where the river came to the sea, but the country between was all chasms and inaccessible cliffs, or else wild, matted jungle coming down to the shore (which was full of quicksands) and that it would take a week's hard travel to get half-way there—that is to say, to the part where it began to be really difficult—which put the lid on that suggestion.

Then Vanderdecken asked if there was any narrow part of the river, and he was told there was one point, some league or so from the town, where the cliffs were not so very wide apart. But to make up for that they were very high, and more than steep because they leaned over the river, which rushed fiercely below almost in darkness, so far down was it. Short of flying over, said the King, there was no way to pass there.

But Vanderdecken asked him to step out on the ground what he thought would be about the distance across, and when this was done he nodded in a satisfied way. Then he asked if there were trees on the farther side, and being told there were many trees on both sides, growing close to the edge of the cliffs he said, "This will be like drinking Schnapps," and (his own words reminding him) took the King in to have some. After a little more conference, he arranged to meet him at the town on the following morning as I have already related.

THE INGENUITY OF VANDERDECKEN

In addition to their weapons and personal belongings the Dutchmen had taken some ship's gear with them. It consisted of the following:

1 long stout rope (spare topsail halyard).
1 coil of thin rope.
1 small anchor (belonging to the longboat).
1 stout iron bar (spare handle of deck pump).
1 strong net of rope (used for hoisting out of the hold).
2 saws.
3 axes.
4 adzes.
1 two-inch auger.
1 big hammer.
1 bag of nails and other small matters.

On arriving at the narrow part of the river, Vanderdecken walked to and fro with his mate, looking at all points. At length he stopped and said, "This is where we get busy."

The opposite cliff was not very far away (possibly about two hundred feet) and there were many trees about, growing close to the edge, as the King had said. Far below could be seen flashes of white where the torrent broke into foam as it roared on in the gloom.

A tall young tree, of a springy character, was cut down and the branches were lopped off. Two sides were then cut away until it looked something like a very long thick plank; the Snergs working at it with great fury, so that the air was full of chips. Then they…

No, on second thoughts I consider it inadvisable to give a detailed description of the device which Vanderdecken made. It would be to turn from a narrative of adventure (with a moral) to a cheap treatise on mechanics. Let it suffice to say that with great labour of all hands he made a fairly good imitation of a Roman balista, which was so useful in inducing besieged peoples to be reasonable by heaving tons of rock at them. This shows the advantage of a classical education.

Instead of rock he was going to heave the anchor, with the rope attached to it and neatly coiled up, to the other side of the river. The other end of the rope was tied to a tree, and all that had to be done was to cut another rope that acted as the trigger of this deadly arrangement.

HOW THEY PASSED OVER THE RIVER

Vankderdecken carefully inspected the completed arrangements and, after warning some enthusiastic Snergs to stand a little further off, drew his cutlass. One dexterous slash and the rope parted, there was a terrific jarr that shook some of the lighter Snergs off their feet, and the anchor flew across the river like an ungainly bird, the rope uncoiling in the air behind it, and crashed into the trees on the opposite side. The Snergs raised a joyful cheer, but the Dutchmen, being phlegmatic, did not. Instead, they grabbed the rope and hauled it in. A dozen pairs of extra hands had it in' a moment, and hauled with a will to the tune of "Fifteen men." The rope grew taut—then slipped. They hauled away, and it caught again— slipped once more, and caught again. And this time it had caught firmly, for all hands were pulling and the rope was as taut as a rod. It was belayed smartly round a tree and lashed securely, and a moment later a Snerg was hanging on to it and going across with swift jerks.

He disappeared in the foliage (the first Snerg to arrive on the other side; he got a decoration for it). A minute later he came running to the edge of the cliff and shouted that all was well; the anchor had caught firmly, with each fluke round a small but sufficient tree trunk. The job was done. Here was a road to the unknown land quite good enough for seamen, and more than good enough for Snergs, who can climb like startled cats.

Vanderdecken expressed his satisfaction at the successful result, for if the anchor trick had proved a failure it would have been necessary to pad a Snerg up with lots of straw and shoot him across with a line attached so that he could haul the rope over after arrival. There was a great deal of resource and determination about this sea captain.

It was waxing late, for the construction of the device had taken the greater part of the day, and there was no time to be lost if they were all to get over before night. The rope was only as thick as a fair-sized broom handle so it was decided that they would have to pass over at long distances apart in order not to put too great a strain on it, but they were told to move in lively fashion. Vanderdecken and the King went first, and then the others—thirty-three Dutch seamen and two hundred and one Snergs (the odd one was the trumpeter)—each carrying his weapons and kit securely lashed to him because the position of travel was of course upside-down, and it was quite dark before the last one got over. Camp fires were soon burning brightly and each man prepared his bed, of chopped-up ferns. Sentries were posted in an orderly way, steel casques and breastplates being compulsory. Then, after a hasty supper, they turned in for the night.

BOOT AND SADDLE

This heading is not quite correct because, though they had boots they had no saddles, but it means that they were off. The trumpet blew a full hour before daybreak, and by the time the dawn came they had had some breakfast and were all ready. King Merse, who had something of Napoleon's ability, left full directions with a crowd of fifty Snergs who had remained for the night on the Snerg side of the river. They were to divide into two lots, one for each side, and the lot on the enemy side was to dig a deep semicircular trench and make a high semicircular wall to defend the point where the rope was anchored. The lots were to change places every third day. And until they saw the Expeditionary Force returning they were to send a daily messenger to the town to say that all was well—meaning that nothing had happened so far—and this message was to be forwarded on to Miss Watkyns by a special runner. It is indeed terrible to think that all this fuss should be caused by the folly and disobedience of two shrimps like Sylvia and Joe.

The force started off in the direction of some rising ground, from which they would be able to reconnoitre the country. Four agile Snergs went some quarter of a mile ahead, and behind came the main body, in fours, led by Vanderdecken and the King. The former wore wide boots with tops like buckets and a sea-cap of fur, and carried a long deadly-looking musket. The latter wore an inlaid cuirass and steel casque and a sword of proof. In his hand he swung a double-edged battle-axe and altogether he looked very serviceable for his size. The Snergs that remained behind watched them marching away into the unknown land, until the trees hid them from view and they could be seen no more, and even the clumping of the Dutchmen's sea-boots died away.

THE FIRST DAY'S MARCH

It was late in the afternoon when the Expeditionary Force halted on a hill and surveyed with interest a little distant cluster of towers. It was the first sign of habitation they had met with in a long, hard march.

Their preliminary inspection of the country in the morning had shown them only gently rolling plains, with patches of dense woods here and there, which seemed to be quite uninhabited, so it was a toss-up which way they should take. Vanderdecken had said that since they did not know the proper course to steer it was best to make one and stick to it; even if it led them away from the lost ones the same might be said of any course, and they had to go somewhere. So they selected sou'west-by-west and tramped it steadily for many hours, marvelling at the strange absence of natives or roads or houses. Nor were there signs of dragons or unicorns or other fierce fauna rumoured to be in the land beyond the river. The fiercest thing they saw was a huge rabbit, with claws; and all that it did was to make a nasty face at them and run away.

The course was changed after a midday rest and they went sou'east-by-south, Vanderdecken having given his opinion that since they had met with nothing to guide them in the search it would be best to go about on the other tack, which means to go zigzag. And so at last they came to the hill-top and saw the distant towers, deep in waving woods. The direction was taken, and they went down and through the trees, and another couple of hours' march brought them to the same compact little stronghold in which, two days before, the wanderers they were searching for had made themselves so much at home.

THE MYSTERIOUS CASTLE AGAIN

King Merse did not leave things to chance. He sent Snergs ahead in pairs, as is advocated by militarists, and the main body came behind. The scouts reported that the castle, though prosperous-looking, did not appear to be a scene of activity. With the exception of smoke coming from what they thought (and hoped) was a kitchen chimney, there was no sign of life about it.

The Dutchmen re-primed their muskets and the Snergs got their bows ready, and all approached and halted by the door in the outer wall; then King Merse ordered his trumpeter to blow the horn which hung outside.

I may mention that it had been decided that, to save time and provisions, the country should be treated as an enemy country until the contrary was proved.

The trumpeter blew (not inaptly) the Snerg equivalent of "Come to the cookhouse door," and after a brief interval a face appeared looking down at them from the wall. It was a fat, pompous face, to which all hands took an instinctive, but perhaps slightly unreasonable, dislike.

"What want ye, my masters?" said the face, looking contemptuously at them.

"It would take too long to tell all we want," replied King Merse, "but just at this moment we want to come in and eat. We will tell you the rest later."

"And that may not be," said the man, "for my lord is away and he has given me strict orders to admit no one except on business."

"But eating is right good business," replied the King. "Come, good fellow, do not keep us waiting."

"I fear you will have to eat elsewhere," the man said. "This castle seems to be getting too popular with vagrants. But two days agone some scurril knaves came in my temporary absence and ate a few scores of eggs and a ham and left me to wash up after them. Be advised, therefore, and go before I become an angered."

King Merse, who was not the sort to waste time in unprofitable chat, turned to his men.

"Burst me open this door," he said.

"Nay, if you be so hardy in your ways," cried the man with a sudden change of tone, "I'll even open to you. But I warn you that my lord is terrible in his wrath."

The door opened and there appeared before them a stout person, wearing a long gown and a chain and carrying a wand of office, who was evidently the steward of the castle. "Ay, terrible," he went on. "If he comes back and finds you here—oh, well, if you won't listen, you won't." He concluded on a peevish note, for the King and Vanderdecken were going ahead of their men towards the wide stone steps that led to the main door of the building, which stood open.

Within they found a commodious hall furnished with long tables and benches, and with a raised dais at the end on which was a table of superior finish and several carved arm-chairs.

"And now, good fellow," said the King, after removing his steel headpiece and seating himself at his ease, "to whom does this castle belong?"

"To the famed Sir Bevis, Lord of the King's marches," replied the steward, who had followed him in and who now seemed to think this a case for discretion. "He guards the land against chance attack from the fierce and cruel Snergs, who live on the other side of the deep river. And now I must ask who you are and why—"

"And now tell me if you have seen two children wandering in these parts, or if you have heard of two children wandering here. They should be with a man of about my size."

"I have seen no dwarf—I mean, no gentleman of your size. But I have seen two children this very morning."

"Where?" demanded the King, starting up.

" In the woods, gathering berries. But perchance it were an error to call them children, for the youngest is sixteen and a stout varlet for his age, and the other is some two years older and has a slight beard. They are the sons of my gossip Hugh, the miller, and idle vagabonds both as I have often said to Hugh and advised him to try what rods will do, for if a child——"

"Forget them," interrupted the King, seating himself again. "Now, good fellow, tell me where your ruler lives, and how far it is from here."

"His Majesty, King Kul lives (as all men should know) at Banrive, which is a day's march from here. And now I must insist——"

"Then we will rest here to-night and leave on that day's march by dawn to-morrow. In the meantime we would eat."

"Nay, fair sir, that I cannot allow. If my lord——"

"We will need," said the King, "some good meaty matter (such as pork) as a groundwork. And as beans go well with pork let there be beans also."

"And some beer," suggested Vanderdecken.

"And some beer of course. So see to it, for we would eat quickly, and rest. And talking of rest, where is your lord's bedchamber?"

"It is here," said the steward, opening a door and displaying a large room with two canopied beds in it. "But I fear I cannot allow you to use my lord's best beds, for if——"

"You take that one," said the King to Vanderdecken, pointing to the largest bed. "It looks very comfortable."

"No," replied Vanderdecken politely, "you take it."

"I should really like you to have it," said the King.

"Let's flip for it," suggested Vanderdecken, producing a piece of eight. "Sudden death."

"Heads!" said the King.

"Tails," said Vanderdecken, displaying the coin. "Sorry, old chap." He got into bed (with his sea-boots on) to see how it felt. "Very nice. We'll have a good sleep to-night anyhow."

They went back to their men and directed proceedings. Some men went out to fetch straw to sleep on, others went to the kitchen and instructed by Vanderdecken's cook (whose soup was the cause of all these adventures) prepared some choice food (he was very good at sea-pie), and drew off many gallons of strong beer to wash it down. The steward followed them about with a pen and ink-horn and a piece of parchment, entering against each item taken what he conceived to be the highest tavern rates. A faithful fellow, but something of an ass.

When the meal was over sentries were posted on the walls and the others lay down on the straw. The King and Vanderdecken retired to their beds after giving orders that they were to be roused an hour before the dawn.

"I say, this is comfort," said Vanderdecken, plumping up a feather pillow. "By the way, let's hope we find those youngsters pretty soon."

"Yes," agreed the King. "Because if we don't, we'll be forced to introduce battle, murder and sudden death into these parts, and I want to avoid that if I can."

HOW GORBO GATHERED MANDRAKES

WHEN at last Gorbo desisted from his damp job of looking for mandrakes, the dawn was breaking. It seemed to him that his back was breaking also, for he had stooped and stooped and pulled at roots almost without pause throughout the dismal night. He rested awhile on a fallen log and tried to rest his spine, taking quick looks behind him at intervals.

It had been a night. Not only were the true mandrakes extremely rare—after hours and hours of search he had only got six that he was pretty sure of—but he had been worried by his surroundings. Leaving out the bats, who were troublesome enough, he had been in continuous doubt of the things that lurked in the black shade of the trees round about, things rather like men, but with little furious faces and big pointed ears and mouths that slobbered, who gibbered and pointed at him in the moonlight. There was one fat pale thing, who if he was not a ghoul was extremely like one, and he had come and sat under a holly bush, staring earnestly at him for hours and hours, and occasionally shrieking with laughter. Gorbo was not superstitious in the ordinary sense of the word, but the night had left him nervy, if I may be allowed the expression; especially as he had been warned not to speak while at the job and he wanted so much to relieve his feelings by saying things. In fact if cold fingers had touched him on the back of the neck while he was resting on the log, I think he would have jumped to quite a height; and I do not blame him, for I know that I should have done very much the same.

However, here he had six mandrakes in the basket and the night was past. He got up and made his way along the trail back to Mother Meldrum's house, and hoped that part of his troubles were over, as she could now get busy with spells and the like, and so get the little doors open. There would be, of course, the wood of twisted trees to pass on the other side; but he had hopes that he would not find this too difficult, since he had learned quite a lot of common sense in the last two or three days and he would apply it. Let him but get to the other side of the river, he thought, and he would soon find a way to get the children safely home.

He called out for Sylvia and Joe as he came near the house; but there was no reply, no running of little feet to greet him. He went quickly to the kitchen door and pushed it open, but there was nobody there. He called again loudly and anxiously, and then a door at the side of the fireplace opened and Golithos came out, stooping almost double to get through.

"Hullo," he said in an unfriendly tone, "what do you want"

"Where are those children?" demanded Gorbo, as soon as he had recovered from his surprise.

"Children? How should I know? I'm not a nursery-maid."

Gorbo dropped his basket and switched his bow round to have it handy.

"Oh, leave that bow of yours alone!" cried Golithos, changing his tone. "You're always making me nervous with the beastly thing. The little ones went away in the night along with the funny man, Mother Meldrum says, and I don't know where they are. How should I?"

"Where's she gone to?" said Gorbo after a miserable moment. "Quick!"

"She ran out to look for them. Oh, do put it down! It's not my fault, is it?"

Gorbo stood with his face all twisted with dismay, staring up at the other. What had happened now? He thought and thought, but could make nothing of it.

"Sit down and make yourself at home," said Golithos after a moment, taking a seat on a stool by the fireplace. "She'll be back soon I expect."

Gorbo sat down after a moment or two and stared at the fire and thought. Golithos looked awkwardly at him from time to time, but did not speak. And so they sat in silence until a brisk step was heard without and Gorbo started up.

The door opened with a crash and Mother Meldrum appeared, looking horribly gaunt and ugly and angry in a long outdoor cloak and a high peaked hat.

"Oh, so you're back, are you?" she said.

"Yes, Mum. But where's Sylvia and Joe?"

"They're gone—the little fools!"

"Gone where?" cried Gorbo.

"You keep civil!" shouted the old woman. " Don't you bellow at me!"

"No, Mum, I won't," said poor Gorbo. "But where have they gone to—please?"

"King Kul will have them by to-night. Them and the funny man. I ran after them when I found they'd gone, but I was just too late. The funny man was on one horse—with his mouth tied up, which shows they've got some sense—and those fool children were each sitting in front of a rider. Now perhaps they're wishing they hadn't run away from old Mother Meldrum."

"Which way did they go?" cried Gorbo, making for the door. "I'll catch them up———"

"Oh, will you? Well, if you think you can catch mounted men when they've got a two hours' start, or if you think you could do anything if you did catch up with them, you're a bigger fool than you look—and that's saying a good deal."

"But—but what did they run away for?" asked Gorbo, struck with a new doubt.

"How do I know? I was sitting talking to this harmless old bunch of nerves" (indicating Golithos) "who'd come to pay me a neighbourly visit, when I thought I'd give a look at them to see that they were quite comfortable. And when I got up there the room was empty and the window was open and they'd gone. And the funny man was gone too. So I just went after them, and got sight of them just too late. King Kul's got them all right. I suppose the funny man told them to go. He's noodle enough for anything. But if you really want to save them, I'll tell you the only way how."

"Oh, thank you, Mum!" exclaimed Gorbo.

"But first I'm going to have breakfast." She threw off her cloak and began clattering the pots and pans about. "I'm not going to starve for those brats."

"If I hadn't been all the night getting those mandrakes," said Gorbo, tearing at his hair, " I wouldn't have lost them. Oh, I am the biggest fool after all! "

"You're near it at any rate." Mother Meldrum had stopped in her work and picked up the basket he had brought. "Is this what you call mandrakes?"

"Yes, Mum," replied Gorbo humbly. "It seemed to me they squeaked a little when I pulled them up."

"Common swamp parsnips!" said Mother Meldrum with bitter scorn, flinging them out of the door. "So that's all the good you are. Yah!"

She turned away and went on with her cooking.

Gorbo sat down and buried his face in his hands. Blow after blow. Not only had he lost the children, but he had lost them while searching throughout a hard disagreeable night for a few worthless specimens of the common swamp parsnip (Avacabolis communis). Life really did not seem worth living to him.

"Liven up!" said the old woman after a while. "I'll show you the way to save them, as I said; you trust to old Mother Meldrum. Meantime you'd better eat."

She dished up a huge platter of kidneys, small sausages and bacon, and an omelette. The exquisite savour of these, together with her proffer of help, brought some cheer to the sore heart of Gorbo and he drew up his stool to the table and ate gratefully. The kidneys were cooked to perfection, the omelette had been made by the hand of an artist. Mother Meldrum was wicked and cruel and ugly and feared by all, but there was that in her which goes far to redeem the character of the vilest—she could cook.

"Golithos only eats grass and such like," she said with a fiendish laugh, "so he can finish up this bit of raw cabbage. Eat hearty, Golithos."

Golithos drew up his stool with a discontented look and picked daintily at the cabbage, eating with his front teeth only as if he had no appetite for it. He looked longingly at the mixed grill, but his fear of Mother Meldrum was great and he kept silent. She told him (while drawing a pot of foaming beer for Gorbo) that he would find all the water he wanted and more in the water-butt outside.

Breakfast being over she sat and considered awhile, casting an occasional glance at Golithos. It was evident that she desired him out of the way; and it is usually a delicate matter to convey to a third person that he is what the French call de trop. But she managed it.

"Golithos," she said suddenly, "get to blazes out of this. Go outside and stay by that tree stump over there so that I can see you're not listening."

Golithos got up and moved blunderingly out of the door and stood where she had told him to, looking sulkily about him.

THE COZENING OF GORBO

"He's a slow-witted one if ever there was one," Mother Meldrum remarked. "You're not much, but you're better than he is. Now what I have to tell you is this. Those children are in deadly peril—now don't start interrupting me, or I'll leave you to settle it yourself. You don't know about King Kul, but I do. If I were to tell you only half the things he's done it would make each one of those coarse hairs of yours stand up, and as that wouldn't be a pretty sight I won't do it. But I'll tell you he's the fiercest and cruellest beast that ever brandished a sceptre. Now the only way to save those children from a horrible fate—at the least having their heads cut off as obtrusive foreigners—is for you to kill him. I'm not counting the funny man at all; he's a goner in any case."

"But—but surely, Mum," said Gorbo in great horror, "no man would kill two harmless little things like them! Why, it simply isn't done!"

The old woman laughed scornfully. "Poor innocent old Foozelum. Why, he does things like that for fun. It's a saying of his that he loves to see a little head bounce off its stalk. Of course you haven't heard about the infants' class at the Sunday School. However, don't let's go into disagreeable details; the main thing is that somebody has got to finish him off. I've tried to get Golithos to do the job, but he hasn't any pluck now and I'm tired of arguing with him. Now, will you do it? Remember it's the only possible way of saving those little ones."

"Yes, Mum," replied Gorbo, springing up. "You just show me the way there and I'll see what I can do with my little bow."

"You needn't trouble about your little bow. In the first place you'd never be able to get through the guards so as to have a shot at him. There's only one way to do it surely, and it's lucky you've got an experienced witch to tell you how."

"I'll do it any way you say, Mum; so long as I can do it quick."

"That's the sort of man I like," she said approvingly. "Just wait here a bit."

She went out, and Gorbo sat in a state of horror and dismay. Here was a terrible result of his fatheadedness ! To know that the innocent little ones were in the power of a tyrant who loved to see small heads bounce off—to know that if he had not tempted them to visit the twisted trees they would have been long ago safe in their own home—to realize that his name would be held for ever in execration among the Snergs as the fool who led the two children to captivity and death! No wonder he bowed his head and moaned in anguish and wept.

Mother Meldrum returned with a long thin bundle under her arm. "Now then, waterworks," she said, in coarse allusion to his tears, "sit up and pay attention for there must be no mistake here."

"Yes, Mum." Gorbo sat up and listened eagerly.

"First, you'll have to get into the King's palace without being seen. And the only way to do that is to wear a cap of invisibility. Here it is" (producing a seedy looking article). "It is seven hundred years old, which accounts for its being a bit out of fashion, but it works all right. Take it and be careful never to put it on until you actually need it, because it only works once with one person. If you were to put it on now you would be invisible for about ten minutes. Then its power—with you—would be gone for ever. Do you understand?"

"Yes, Mum. You mean I must only use it when I get into the palace."

"You've got it. You're improving a bit. Now the next thing is this." She produced a long whippy sapling and swished it in the air.

"Yes, Mum. And what do I do with that?"

"This," she said impressively, "is a sword of sharpness. The instant you smite with it it turns into a sword, and any person you smite will be cut into two halves. It belonged originally to a cousin of Queen Mab; he used it to clear up some family trouble. But remember that when you have smitten it once it becomes a sapling again and its power goes for ever—that is, as far as you are concerned."

"Yes, Mum. You mean that if I swot the King with it he will be cut into two bits."

"That's it. And it will look rather well; sorry I won't be there to see it. Now when you have done this there will probably be more than a little excitement and it will be advisable for you to get out of the way for a time. You see when the tyrant is dead the people will rise up in their power and celebrate by freeing all the unhappy prisoners and so forth, and that, of course, will save those dear little children. But you had better go for a little run."

"Yes, Mum. But how do I manage it?"

"These" (producing a very shabby pair of slippers) "are shoes of swiftness. The moment you have done the deed, slip these on and run. But I advise you not to run too much or you may find yourself in Mesopotamia or in the middle of the ocean or somewhere. Just a few brisk steps will be enough, and even then it will take you half the night to walk back, because these, like the cap and sword, only work once. When you get back again you will be hailed as a great and good man and the dear little things will be delivered over to you safe and sound. Also your friend the funny man, if you really need him. So here's everything, nicely wrapped up. Do exactly as I've told you, and remember that if you make a mess of it, the children's ghosts will haunt you—carrying their little heads under their arms"

"I'll start now," cried Gorbo, taking the bundle containing the wonderful treasures and his bow and other matters and making for the door. "Just tell me the road."

"Turn to the left when you get out of the wood and go along the green drive for a mile or two. Then you'll hit the high road which leads straight to the town. So go to it!"

Gorbo thanked her briefly but fervently and darted off down the path. Mother Meldrum watched him disappear in the trees and then went back and sat down and laughed until she shook with horrid merriment.

A FEARFUL BARGAIN

After a few minutes' enjoyment of her secret jest she called to Golithos to approach, and he came in looking very sulky and seated himself.

"Where have you sent that Snerg to?" he asked.

"Ah," she replied, "that's telling." And she went on chuckling.

"Now," she said after a time, "let's get to business. Are you going to take my offer or not? I may as well warn you (if you haven't found it out yet) that I'm a bit short-tempered, and if you get obstinate with me I've ways of making all kinds of trouble for you. I'm not an experienced witch for nothing."

Golithos scratched his head in a discontented way. "It's so dangerous," he said at length.

"So it is to make me annoyed. Now then, answer up! Will you kill the King if I get those young ones for you?"

"But you haven't got them to give."

"Yah! I can get them back easily enough if I make up my mind to do it—and if you make it worth my while."

"Yes, but—but why didn't you get that Snerg to kill him. He's fool enough."

"Yes, he is—a bit worse than you in some ways, and that's why I sent him out of the way. But the reason is that I've found out by black magic that if the King is killed at all it will be done by an ogre, and you're the only one left in these parts. So now you know."

"Oh! So that's it, is it?—And does your magic say what will happen to the ogre?"

"Yes, it says he'll live happy ever after."

Golithos scratched his head again. In spite of his belief in Mother Meldrum he had doubts whether she was telling the exact truth here.

"I suppose I must do it," he muttered sullenly. "But I want to be sure of those little ones first. You bring them here and keep them safe for me first. Then I'll go and do it."

The old woman glared furiously at him. "Yes, you're trying to get me annoyed," she said. "Very well, then, I'll show you."

"No, wait, please! You see if I could just see them it would put me in such good heart for the job. I've been living on lettuce and stuff like that so long that I'm not as brave as I was; and though I've eaten my cow it doesn't encourage me like my own natural food. You must see that. It's so reasonable."

She looked at him partly in rage and partly in doubt. "H'm!" she sniffed, "you're the flabbiest thing in ogres I've ever met, and I've met a few in my time. Do you mean to say that if I'd shown them to you this morning you'd have done the King in?"

"Yes," he replied eagerly, "that's it. Just a glimpse of those nice little well-filled-out children—which you promised me so faithfully—would have made me quite anxious to do it. But I never even got a peep at them," he went on pathetically. "You must own it's hard on me."

"I'll get even with the funny man," growled Mother Meldrum. "Well, suppose I bring them both back? Will you go straight off at once as soon as you've had a look at them and do what I want?"

"Oh, yes! I'll just have one good look at them and I'll go at once. Of course if I could have a piece of one first, just to encourage me properly, so to speak———"

"Well, you won't. You'll see them when I've got them safely here and then you'll be off, or you'll see what I'm like when really annoyed. Did you bring your axe with you?"

"Yes, I've got it here." He went to a corner of the kitchen and produced a mighty battle-axe and balanced it in his hand. "Many's the stout man-at-arms I've laid out with this in the old days."

"The days when you had some pluck, you mean."

"Yes, that's it. But my pluck's coming back. And if you give me a nice roast pig for dinner, it'll come back more. And when I see those dear little children waiting for me, it'll fix it for keeps." His eyes were rolling and his teeth were showing fiercely now, and he handled the axe, which any other man could scarcely lift, as if it were a medium-sized chopper.

"Yes," said Mother Meldrum, after watching him for a moment, "I think that's the way it will have to be. I see you need some practical encouragement, being the worm you are, so wait here until I come back with them. Keep your courage up by thinking about them. It's taken a long time to work you up to this, Golithos," she went on with a fierce laugh, "but I think I've done it at last. You'll get what you want, and I'll get that I want—Revenge!"

She sprang up and did a hideous dance of joy round the kitchen, footing it with an agility that seemed marvellous considering her years. Golithos, whose long dormant savagery was awakening fast, laughed long and boisterously. Truly a terrible scene. Let us not linger over it.

CAPTIVES ON THE ROAD

It is fortunate for children (and for grown-ups too if they can manage it) when they do not concern themselves greatly about the future possibilities of a calamity. Sylvia and Joe were of this kind—especially Joe—and what chiefly troubled them as they rode along in front of their guards was the separation from their friend Gorbo, who if he could not have actually saved them from this happening, would at least have been comfort to them on the road; the fact that they were being carried captives to a monarch of whom they had heard distressing accounts seemed less of an evil, for its troubles were connected with the future, and the future is always some distance ahead.

They were not treated badly, and they were allowed to talk with the men-at-arms with whom they rode, but in a low voice because otherwise it would have been bad for discipline. Baldry rode at some distance from them so they got no chance to speak to him. The leader had allowed him to go unmuzzled after a time on the condition that he did not talk, and Baldry passed the time singing quietly to himself songs about cruel fate and other melancholy subjects. He had evidently resigned himself to whatever might befall.

The leader—whose name they learned was Sir Giles—asked the children some questions as to how they came to be with the King's jester, but though they answered him truthfully and told him all about Watkyns Bay (which he had never heard of) and the Snergs (of whom he had heard very little and that little not good) and their strange adventures, he could make nothing of it; and he finally said that it defeated him entirely and that abler heads than his must solve the mystery.

As they went on the country became rather more populated; there were farms and windmills and so forth, and here and there a small castle or moated grange. They halted for about half an hour at an inn to rest the horses and have breakfast; Sir Giles told the host to send the bill in to the Chancellor of the Exchequer. Sylvia and Joe had each a plate of little hot fish, rather like sardines, and a bowl of milk, and this cheered them up greatly. Baldry interrupted his sad crooning to eat two chops and drink a pot of ale. Then he went on with a new song about his being Fortune's toy. Baldry wanted some understanding.

It was well on in the afternoon when they came round the corner of a thick wood and saw the town close at hand. It reminded the children of a picture of a mediæval town on a coloured calendar that Miss Scadging had brought from London last year. The houses had heavy crossed timbers and high pitched roofs, and the streets were paved with huge cobble stones like grey footballs. They passed through a gate with big towers and by quaint little shops and taverns where people sat outside on benches and drank out of large pots, or else leaned against posts. There seemed to be a good deal of spare time in the town, and people came clustering round to stare at the children; but when Baldry was recognized (he had for some reason seated himself facing the horse's tail as soon as they reached the town) there was great excitement, and they called other people to come and see. But Sir Giles ordered them to stand back like good fellows and make way for the King's men, and the procession went clattering down the street until it halted in the courtyard of the royal palace.

It was indeed an anxious moment for Joe and Sylvia as they were lifted down and led through into a lofty hall. At first they had only a confused impression of brilliant costumes and high pointed head-dresses of ladies and the crimson legs of small pages and general gorgeousness. Compared to the palace of King Merse II this was as a house in Park Lane, W. is to a maisonnette in Poplar, E., and they felt very small and untidy and of no importance at all as they went with Sir Giles (Sylvia carrying the puppy) through these high-class surroundings and halted before a throne on which was seated one who wore a kingly crown. At last they were in the presence of the dreaded monarch.

KING KUL I

It would be well here to point out to my readers (and especially the younger ones) that rumour is more often contradicted than confirmed by experience, and to enlarge on the moral conveyed. The reason against my doing so at length is the fear that I may become a little tedious, so I will merely state that, to the great surprise and relief of the children, there were no signs of ruthlessness about the King.

He was of great girth and he had a flowing grey beard, and in these particulars he bore out Baldry's description of him. But his expression was one of benevolence and good humour and he smiled on the children with what, if it had not been blent with a touch of native majesty, might have been described as a sort of fatuous fatherliness.

He was richly though tastefully arrayed. His doublet was of three (or four) piled velvet, green and embroidered with gold, and his hose were shrimp pink, a colour he much affected. From his shoulders hung a sky-blue robe lined with ermine, and the crown on his partially bald head was decorated with fine repoussé work. Never had the children conceived such magnificence in a man's dress, and they stared in wonder and admiration.

"Welcome, Sir Giles," he said, ignoring Baldry, who went down on his knees beside the children. "Tell me who are these little ones and how came you to bring them together with this rudesby."

" 'Rudesby' is rather good," observed Baldry in an interested tone.

"I found them travelling with the knave, sire," replied Sir Giles. "And as I could not leave them alone in the forest I brought them also. But I can make nothing of their tale, sire. It appears to me such as might be told by a minstrel who had been too long at the wine-pot. A tale of a certain Countess Watkyns in that terror-haunted land beyond the deep river, and of many millions of other children, and of Snergs who are friendly with them. I leave it to your Majesty to judge, for I can make nothing of it."

"Ah, you're slow, that's what's the matter," remarked Baldry.

"Silence, thou villain!" roared the King.

Baldry clapped both hands over his mouth with a look of extreme terror.

"Snergs, did you say?" went on the King. "Could it be possible that these little innocents know aught of that fierce and cruel race?"

"Please, sir," said Joe, who felt that he must defend his friends, holding up one hand according to the custom of Watkyns Bay in class time. "Please, sir, we're all very fond of the Snergs. They're not fierce at all."

"Not fierce, say you, little man! Nay, that passes understanding. There must be more in this than meets the eye."

"You mean the ear, of course," said Baldry.

"Remove me this pestilent ass!" cried the King. "We will judge his case at a fitter time."

Four men-at-arms surrounded the jester and, at a word of command from Sir Giles, marched out with him. His really incredible folly caused him to drop on all fours and go out creeping swiftly between them; doubtless he gathered some encouragement from the smothered laughter of the more thoughtless courtiers.

Put to some extent at his ease by the King's kind manner, Joe told the tale of their wanderings and adventures. He explained as well as he could and with Sylvia's assistance, the way of living at Watkyns Bay, the general nature of the country beyond the deep river, and the amiable character of the Snergs, with whom the Society lived on such satisfactory terms. The King listened in deep wonder.

"Can it be," he said, turning to the court, "that we have been in ignorance of the true nature of things beyond the river?—that we have accepted without question the traditions handed down to us, and are now to be corrected by these babes? Can it be———" He went on moralising in most approved fashion, and the courtiers made acquiescing murmurs, as was expected of them.

"But one thing is clear," he went on. "We must pay instant attention to this Golithos, who appears to give indications of becoming a menace, and also to Mother Meldrum. She has had a good deal of rope in the past, and perchance it is the time to give her a bit more, though in a different sense of the word. They must be brought here for judgment at once. That shall be your next job, Sir Giles."

"Oh, very well, sire," replied Sir Giles, but not very heartily.

"And that reminds me," said the King. "Your betrothed, the Lady Ermyntrude, can look after these little ones, for the hour is late, and we would have them to sit at our evening meal. So fair damsel," he continued to a young lady standing nearby, "take charge of this little golden-haired maid and this sturdy male infant and see that they be given a change of raiment and also (for they are a bit grubby) the refreshment of the bath."

The young lady, who was richly dressed, and extremely pretty (her one defect was a touch of indefinable sauciness) came forward and curtseyed. She then gave a hand to each of the children and led them forth.

A CHANGE OF CLOTHES AT LAST

With the assistance of a couple of maids, Sylvia and Joe were soon tubbed and scrubbed and then seated, each wrapped in a sheet, awaiting the decision of the Lady Ermyntrude, who took clothes seriously. In time she selected what she considered suitable from the royal wardrobe (things that the royal children had grown out of) and began to dress them up. When she had finished with them the effect was startling. Sylvia had on a dress of white silk adorned with flowers and bees worked in gold, and little red shoes with pom-poms on them. Her hair was all fluffed-out beneath a snow-white cap like a sugar loaf leaning backwards. Joe had a bright crimson doublet and hose and a cap with a white feather on it. His shoes wanted some getting used to for the toes were so pointed and long that they had to be fastened to his knees with tiny gold chains. In his belt he had a little dagger in an embroidered sheath, and this he liked more than anything. He told Sylvia that he had told her all along that things would come out all right and that she needn't worry.

"What do you think of Sir Giles?" asked the Lady Ermyntrude when the children's toilet was complete and they were sitting opposite to her on two footstools.

"He's not bad," replied Joe. (After all, Sir Giles had looked after them pretty well and given them breakfast.)

"He's bossy," said the lady (not the word she used of course, but the nearest I can get to it).

"Is he, Miss?" Sylvia asked.

"Yes, with most people. But not with me." Here she laughed scornfully.

"You're going to marry him, aren't you, Miss—I mean, my Lady?" asked Sylvia timidly.

"In August."

"Oh, so soon?" Sylvia got greatly interested. "Bridesmaids?"

"Six. Would you like to see my wedding-dress—as far as it's gone?"

"I should love it!"

So Joe had to wander about the room for half an hour while these two thoroughly feminine females went into close details.

ANOTHER MEAL WITH ROYALTY

The evening meal was a matter of some ceremony and observance of old customs. The public was admitted in moderate numbers on payment of a small fee (which went to the poor) and it was quite the thing for people who wanted to give country friends a treat to take them to the palace in order to see from behind a railed-off space the royal party feeding. Those who came on this particular evening had no reason to complain that they had not had their money's worth.

The jovial character of the King made him sometimes impatient of ceremony, and once the trumpets had sounded to announce that he had removed his outer robe and taken his seat, he would adopt a free and easy manner calculated to put nervous guests at their ease. I do not mean that Joe and Sylvia were nervous. They had been guests of honour at the table of King Merse II and knew something of the ways of courts—though this of course was on a much more magnificent scale—and, in addition, they were upheld by the consciousness that they were fitly attired. Those who know—as I confess I do—the great gain in ease and self-respect due to a new suit of clothes will readily understand this.

While the meal proceeded the King expressed sympathy with them for their mislaying of Gorbo and comforted them by saying that he would undoubtedly turn up safe and sound. He said he would have inquiries made at once.

"It is indeed a gratification," he said, "to hear that the Snergs are nice and harmless and not at all fierce. I must try and arrange some way of meeting their king, who I have no doubt is a very worthy man in his way. It would be to clear up the misunderstandings of ages. And I should especially like to see your faithful friend Gorbo. I trust I shall shortly. In the meantime," he went on with hospitable smiles, "have another of these, Sylvia" (handing her a plate of confections rather like muffins with fruit inside). "Little girls should build up their systems with plenty of food, and these are full of vitamines."

"Thank you, sire," said Sylvia, taking one.

"But these are cold," went on the King as he bit into another. "Let me give you a hot one." Then, for as I have said he despised ceremony in small things, he rose and reached for a huge silver dish (with a hot water arrangement beneath it) where the muffins were heaped.

I ask you to note that, the dish being at some distance from him, he leant forward until he was almost prone on the table, the muffin he had bitten to test its temperature being still between his teeth.

A STINGER

At that instant fearful shouts were heard, and to the bewildering surprise and joy of Sylvia and Joe, they saw Gorbo bounding up the hall. He wore instead of his close-fitting Snerg cap, a strange one of filthy appearance. In his left hand he bore a pair of ragged shoes, and in his right he held aloft a long whippy sapling.

He did not see them; even if he had he would not have recognized in these splendidly-dressed children his travel-stained young friends; he had eyes only for the alleged tyrant whose gold crown revealed his identity and whose attitude as he leaned across the table was excellent for the user of a magic sword. He leapt forward—remember all this occupied but one or two seconds—and brought the sapling down on the King's person with a juicy smack that rang through the hall.

To say merely that things moved briskly after this is to confess—as I must—inability to cope in words with so strange a situation. I will, however, do my best to give a general impression of subsequent happenings.

The King bounced upright—nay, more than upright—and with eyes goggling and utterance impeded by the muffin in his mouth, glared maniacally at his assailant. And all present were so paralysed with amazement that for an instant there was utter silence. O moments big as years!

The thoughts of Gorbo in that bitter speck of time might be expressed as follows:

"I have been cozened. This cap is not a cap of invisibility, because everybody is looking at me. This sapling is not a sword of sharpness, because just look at what's happened! Therefore, for the love of Mike, let these be shoes of swiftness, for I need them!"

He flung away the sapling, sprang into the shoes, and ran.

He ran into the arms of about twenty soldiers, each of whom grabbed a bit of him somewhere.

"It's Gorbo!" cried Sylvia in agony. "Oh, poor old Gorbo!"

"Gorbo, is it?" roared the King, sweeping away with his arms those who rushed to tend him, and literally gnashing his teeth. "So that's your Gorbo? Harmless, eh? Not fierce at all! Oh————!"

Here I must cease writing down his words.

THE MORNING AFTER

When the children woke next day the events of the evening came to them with a shock. They had not been thrown into a dungeon, as they had not unreasonably feared would be the case, but had been rather hurriedly bundled out of the way by the Lady Ermyntrude and put to bed in a fairly comfortable back room with two beds and told to go to sleep at once, which they felt was rather a difficult thing to do under the circumstances. They felt that they were losing their popularity, and besides, they were greatly worried about their friend. Speculation as to why he had behaved as he had and what would be his probable fate kept them whispering for hours.

But when they were dressed by a maid (who brought them an early cup of milk) and had gone downstairs, they found the situation easier. The King had passed a good night. He had no temperature and was able to eat a hearty breakfast. He did not express a wish to see the children, and they were glad of this because they felt it would have been so awkward. The Lady Ermyntrude gave them their breakfast and then took them out for a walk in the garden, and Tiger had a run with some puppies that belonged to her.

The King attended a council at which were discussed various suggestions made by the nobles as to the ceremonies to be observed in the cutting off of Gorbo's head. It was finally decided that it should be done in the market-place at 11.30, and, this being settled, the King proposed (for the basis of his method of government was strict justice) that the villain should receive a fair trial.

Gorbo was brought in, loaded with an almost unnecessary length of chain, and stood before the Lord Chancellor, who was to conduct the case.

"Your name, prisoner?" asked the Lord Chancellor.

"Gorbo, so please you, sir," replied the unhappy Snerg.

"Your age, Gorbo?"

"Two hundred and seventy-three, sir."

"Your occupation, Gorbo?"

"Potter, sir."

"And why, Gorbo, did you leave the harmless calling of potting to come to this land and give a fleshy cut to the King's Grace?"

"Because————" He could say no more.

"The reason is inadequate, Gorbo. Think, for your time on earth is short if you give no better bid for life."

"Mother Meldrum told me to," said Gorbo, his wits roused by the extremity.

"Aha, now we get near it! But even then, Gorbo, the reason seems no full one. Is it the foul custom of the Snergs to smite all, however exalted, at the chance word of a witch?"

"She—she said that the King was a grievous tyrant—and that he needed killing badly. But the chief reason was she said that if I didn't kill him, he'd kill Sylvia and Joe."

The Lord Chancellor turned to the King. "In truth, sire, we seem to have secured, at the cost of a stinger to your Majesty's person, the biggest numskull the world has ever known."

"It would seem so," agreed the King, with a half pitying look at Gorbo. "I suggest, my lords, that he be allowed to tell his tale in his own fashion and we will then see if it agrees in substance with the tale of those little ones."

"A noble idea and worthy of your Majesty's brain capacity," said the Lord Chancellor. "Come, fellow, your tale, plainly told."

With much faltering and stammering (for he feared he had proved the truth of the prophecy that he was the biggest fool) Gorbo began his account of all that had happened since he left Watkyns Bay. He warmed up as he proceeded and got more at his ease, for he saw that all listened with deep interest. He diplomatically stopped at the point where he arrived at the palace gates on the previous evening.

"All agrees well with the tale of the children," said the King. "I think, my lords, we must let this oaf keep his head for the present."

"Yes, sire," said the Lord Chancellor, "and in my opinion————"

But his opinion was lost to the world, for at that instant there was heard a clamour without and a sounding knock at the door.

THE INVASION

The door opened smartly and the Captain of the City Guard appeared framed in the doorway, a stoutly-built man in a full suit of mail, with a beard like a pound of coarse-cut tobacco and a rough but not unkindly face.

"My liege," he said, making a leg, "pray pardon my pushing in, but a strange armed force has appeared suddenly, demanding the surrender of the two foreign children and the Snerg."

"An armed force, fellow!" cried the King with justifiable anger. "Demanding of me—I mean us! You are surely talking through your morion."

"Nay, sire, it is but too true. Some two score of large men in quaint boots and some ten score or more of small dwarfish men who may be Snergs. They say that if the three they demand be given to them uninjured they will go in peace."

The King rose to the occasion with true dignity. "Admit them to the City," he said. "We will talk with their leader."

"Well, sire," said the Captain of the Guard, with a not unnatural embarrassment, "the fact is, they have admitted themselves. You see, it happened that I was athirst, and——"

"We will look into that later," interrupted the King with a stern look. "In the meantime, invite this force into our hall as soon as I have taken my seat on the throne."

AN HISTORIC MEETING

The force was drawn up in an orderly way in the hall; Snergs on the right flank, four deep, and the Dutchmen on the left flank. Vanderdecken knew something of the art of war—so useful to seamen of his day—and he had trained his crew to do some simple military exercises, including musketry drill. On the whole the Expeditionary Force, with Snergs in half armour and the sailors carrying their muskets at the slope, looked hard and efficient.

King Kul left his throne and advanced six steps. King Merse came forward, looking every inch a king, though small.

"Welcome, our cousin of Snerg."

Their hands met. King Kul took the arm of the other and led him to a seat by the throne. There was a murmur of satisfaction from the assembled courtiers, while the two exchanged the friendly, but not necessarily very deep, remarks which characterize the conversation of princes or presidents who meet for the first time.

It is of course not very probable that any of my readers will visit this land, but if by chance they should do so I recommend them to take special note of the fresco which was painted to commemorate this historic scene, for it well repays inspection. It is in the vaulted corridor on the left of the hall, next to the cloak-room.

NECESSARY EXPLANATIONS

Formalities were soon over, and King Kul ordered that the two children be brought to greet their friends. In the meantime, he stood, his hands lightly clasped behind him, talking to Vanderdecken, who had been presented to him with due ceremony and whose sterling qualities he could both discern and appreciate. Though but (a merchant adventurer Vanderdecken was of good family; he had as we know some knowledge of the classics, he spoke easily and well, there was no hesitation or mauvaise honte about the man; though his dress was rough and perhaps ill-fitted to the brilliant scene, he bore himself with proper pride. As the late Lord Buscoe said to one who expostulated with him for coming to dinner in plus-fours, you cannot disguise a gentleman.

Sylvia and Joe, in their fine and fancy garb, were brought into the hall by the Lady Ermyntrude and affectionately greeted and kissed by King Merse. They instantly told him that he must demand the release of Gorbo, for he had been put in a dungeon.

"By the way, your Majesty," said King Merse, turning to his brother monarch, " what about my subject, Gorbo? I hear he is in trouble."

"You shall see him," replied the other with a touch of sternness (with two kings conversing the reader will have sometimes to judge their identity by the matter of their speech). "Ho there! bring hither that fellow!"

Metallic sounds caused all to look towards the council chamber where Gorbo had been left with his guards. He came forward, carrying his chain with difficulty and occasionally stumbling over it. He looked at his liege lord with a sheepish smile.

"Hail, Gorbo," said King Merse, amid a deep silence.

"May your shadow ever be a wide one," murmured Gorbo.

"You seem to have got tangled up with some iron, Gorbo. What is it this time?"

Gorbo gave no reply, but only toyed with a link of his chain.

"Let me ask you, our cousin," said King Kul impressively. "Suppose an utter stranger were to come into your hall unannounced and hand you one of the very best with a stout sapling while you were reaching across your own supper-table, what would you say?"

King Merse thought diligently for a moment; then he shook his head. "I give it up," he said. "But," he added half-unconsciously touching the hilt of his sword, "I might be able to tell you what I would do, if that is of any use to you."

"Exactly!" said King Kul; "that is just my point. This subject of yours did so behave to us. And you can scarcely credit what a stinger he gave us. I ask you."

"Well, Gorbo," said King Merse after a serious pause, "to put it in the very mildest way, you are not improving. Can you make anything of this strange case?" he asked of Vanderdecken.

Vanderdecken did not reply in words; he merely grasped his beard and shook his head slowly from side to side as one who is utterly defeated.

"I suppose," went on King Merse, "it were too much to expect that the fellow had some dim shadow of a reason, at the back of what for want of a better word we must call his brain, for this outrage?"

"Oh, we have found reason enough!" cried King Kul, with a slight tendency to rave. "He did it, he says, to save these little children from execution at our hands! These—these whom we were at the moment stuffing with muffins! Oh——" here his sense of the bitter indignity overcame him again and he could only articulate words which I prefer to represent by dashes.

"This is a blow to me," said King Merse, sadly. "I had hoped that when I found Gorbo I would also find that his mind had been broadened by foreign travel; it is said to have that effect. But what hope now?"

"It's all very well," said Gorbo sullenly, "but if you'd eard what Golithos said about the King, and what Mother Meldrum said about him, perhaps you'd have made a little mistake too. And Baldry said——" here he stopped suddenly, for Baldry was his sworn friend and he felt that to go on would not be cricket.

"Baldry!" exclaimed King Merse. "Ah, now the matter is clearing. Tell me what that reprobate said about me."

But Gorbo remained silent.

"Bring hither our one-time jester," said the King to an officer. "I think, cousin, we may find some extra reason for this matter."

BALDRY'S SENTENCE

Baldry was brought in, chewing a straw. There were straws sticking in his hair and more on his clothes. He stood before the King with his eyes cast down and his hands clasped before him, a dejected figure.

"Thou insolent!" said the King, after regarding him for a moment. "Thou impertinent one! Think not to trick me by this show of sorrow. Tell me, have you said aught to this stranger that would lead him to believe me a tyrant?"

Baldry took the straw from his mouth, dried it carefully and deposited it within the bosom of his doublet. He placed his hand daintily over his mouth and coughed a little cough. Then he spoke:

"My liege lord and master, it is true that I did in some sort induce my dear friend Gorbo to believe you more despotic than is perhaps the case. But in my defence I must say that I had some good reason for it, namely, to wit"—here he checked off the items on his fingers—"Firstly, the idea occurred to me a choice one. Secondly, it seemed to be full of humour. Thirdly, I was highly amused at it. Fourthly, it tickled me greatly. Fifthly——"

"Silence me that lewd mouth!" cried the King to the jailor. A kerchief was hastily whipped round Baldry's mouth and held while they waited further orders.

"Listen to my words," said the King sternly, "for you will hear but few again. We can pardon much levity in a professional fool, but this more than reaches the limits of our patience. Go forth from our presence and from our palace and from our City—and keep on going. Know all," he continued, turning to the court, "that Baldry is henceforth exiled from our dominions."

Baldry started violently and stared at him as if he could not comprehend. Then, as the bitter truth dawned upon him, he turned, and with bowed head, paced slowly forth. But after some four or five steps he paused, placing his hand upon his heart as if with a sudden pang. Then, raising his hands aloft with a gesture of despair, he swayed, and fell at full length on his face, as falls a tree.

There was general consternation, and all rushed forward. One, skilled in leechcraft, knelt down and, bending his head sideways, listened carefully. Then he rose. "I cannot hear his heart beat," he said sadly. " He is dead."

They made way for the King, from whose countenance the stern look had faded, giving place to one of deep sorrow. He stood looking down at the prostrate figure and heaved a deep sigh, almost a groan. At length he spoke—in blank verse, for nothing less could express his bitter feelings:

"Alas, poor fool! is't thus that comes the end,
The terminus of all your antic ways?
Could not the fate which spares the grim tom-cat
That yesternight did rack my harmless slumbers,
Making the moonlight tremble with his yells,
Have spared thee too? Can'st ne'er again
Devise thy lightsome jests, thy bonnetings,
Thy traps of booby poised on half-op'd door,
Or juggle with the table furnishings?
No, thou art dead, and I without my fool
Am left to mourn the law inscrutable
That gives us chiefly what we would not have.
The violet withers while the rhubarb thrives,
The buttered slice falls ever upside-down.
The horse we back does seldom find a place,
The horse we back not comes a romping in.

Too late, poor fool, this unavailing woe!
I loved thee more than thou did'st ever know."

"Then in that case," said Baldry, turning smartly over on to his back, "why are you making things so difficult?"

ROYAL CLEMENCY

It was characteristic of Baldry that he always (in seafaring phrase) sailed pretty close to the wind, and it was lucky for him in this case that the King's satisfaction in knowing that he was not dead after all slightly outbalanced his new rage at finding that not only had he been tricked, but that he had wasted some rather superior blank verse. But Baldry dexterously twisted himself out of reach of the King's itching foot and fled to where Sylvia and Joe were standing (both rather perplexed with these happenings) and embraced them with ardour.

"Ah, our cousin of Snerg!" said the King with a mournful smile, "well has the poet said that beneath a monarch's crown there is often a sore head. But now let me recount to you what other reasons this Gorbo of yours gave for his behaviour. It will take some believing."

King Merse, after hearing full details of how Gorbo had been cozened into perpetration of the outrage, gave his opinion that, the man being the ass he was, it would be best to pass the matter over as an error of judgment.

"That's one way of looking at it," said King Kul rather peevishly. "Of course it was I who got the stinger, not you. But," he added with true nobility, " the quality of mercy is not strained like cabbage. Ho there, guards! unchain that extraordinary person. He is free."

Gorbo's fetters were instantly removed and carried away in a basket. He murmured some inarticulate thanks to the King and then went over to his brother Snergs, who were ranged against the wall and who greeted him with affection mingled with scarcely dissembled mirth. But he was cheered by the sudden impact of two small bodies; Sylvia and Joe had flung themselves at him and were hugging him tight.

King Kul watched the scene for a moment with a benevolent smile; then he turned to King Merse and Vanderdecken.

"Come," he said, "to my privy chamber, where a stoup of wine and a mixed biscuit awaits us. The Master of the Buckhounds will see to it that your men are cared for. Pray mind the step."

THE NEXT DAY

The next day passed happily and to the contentment of all except Sir Giles, who instead of walking for hours in the gardens with the Lady Ermyntrude, as he hoped to do, had to mount and away in order to bring Golithos and Mother Meldrum up for judgment. He started early and went off at great speed with his men. Since the job had to be done he would get it over quickly.

The Snergs and the Dutchmen were well entertained by the townspeople. They visited some public places, such as the building of Science and Arts, and were present at the ceremony of unveiling a new horse-trough in the market-place. A good spread, at which the Mayor presided, was given to them in the Town Hall.

Sylvia and Joe enjoyed themselves to the full. They went out shopping with the Lady Ermyntrude, who needed some lining and a piece of narrow insertion, and they roamed about with Gorbo afterwards and each bought a little china mug and saucer as a souvenir. They were very happy for it had been on the whole a most successful and interesting expedition; though they were to start on the homeward journey on the next day but one (a Snerg had been sent post haste to let Miss Watkyns know they were safe) and they would have preferred to stop a little longer, they were also looking forward to the time when they would be back with the other children and telling them all about it. And they really wanted to know what Miss Watkyns and the other ladies would think of it all.

There was a ball that night at the palace. Among those present were Joe and Sylvia, but only for a short time because the. King said they were too young for dissipation. They went to sleep, soothed by the distant music of rebecs, psalterys and viols de gamboys. Truly a happy time.

AND THE DAY AFTER THAT

"Aha!" said King Kul, striking his hands lightly together as he glanced round the breakfast table, "what good things have we to eat this morning? I see kidneys—kippers—a dressed ham—pies of various sorts. Come, our cousin of Snerg, let me recommend the grouse pie."

"Thank you," replied King Merse, helping himself to a good deal. "Are grouse plentiful here?"

"Very plentiful. When you come again we must get up some hawking parties. Mynheer Vanderdecken, this wine is a good breakfast vintage. Let me fill your goblet—But where are our little guests? I heard their merry prattle from my window long ago, when I was having my early hippocras and sandwich."

Before anyone could answer, the Lady Ermyntrude came rushing into the hall holding her skirts some six inches from the ground to facilitate her movements.

"Sire," she panted, "the children cannot be found! I left them about an hour ago in order to powder my—I mean to arrange my coiffure—and they have gone!"

"Gone where?" exclaimed both monarchs, rising to their feet.

"Alas, I cannot say. The household varlets have searched the gardens and called to them, but they cannot be found. The guards at the palace gates have not seen them pass. But they are lost!"

"Tut, tut!" said King Kul, "that seems impossible. They are playing some prank on you. Have you searched the herbaceous borders?"

"Yes, sire, everywhere. But they cannot be found."

Amid general consternation the Captain of the Gate was sent for and came on the run, bolting a crust and brushing crumbs from himself.

"Come, come!" said the King angrily, "you must learn to eat in your own time. We like not this munching in our presence. Now tell me if those children passed the gates this morning."

The Captain made an effort and bolted what was left of the crust. "No, sire," he replied. "Only serving-men have passed in or out on your Majesty's affairs. They and one old man."

"What manner of old man?"

"Of very indifferent manner, sire. He came early this morning to offer fat boiling fowls for your Majesty's kitchen. He had a thin grey beard and he wore a high peaked hat and a cloak and he rode an ass."

"That does not help us very much," remarked the King, pondering deeply.

"Not at all, sire. We were glad to see him pass out, for when he had sold his fowls he brought forth bagpipes from under his cloak and played most execrable music. He went out a-riding his ass, with his feet disposed on his two covered baskets that hung on either side, and there were none that did not stop their ears as he passed. My own ears still ding with the fearsome squealing."

"Enough of this old man and your ears," said the King impatiently. "Now let my soldiers search———"

He was interrupted by the sudden appearance of Gorbo, who darted out from the throng and flung out his arms before him.

"It's Mother Meldrum!" he cried. "The old man was Mother Meldrum! She's got them after all!"

"Got them where?" roared the King and a few other people.

"In the baskets! She popped them in the baskets and played bagpipes so that people wouldn't hear them screaming! Oh!"—here he flung his cap on the ground and jumped on it and tore his hair.

There was a momentary silence of astonishment. That Gorbo, already widely known in these parts as the prize fool of the strange race of Snergs, should find the solution of the mystery came as a bit of a shock. King Merse stared at him as if he were experiencing something of a miracle.

"He is right," exclaimed King Kul. "If this toss-pot and muncher had had the sense to see what is plain to us all" (he forgot that he hadn't seen it himself until it was shouted at him) "those children would not be now in the power of that wretch. Let no one rest until they are found, or avenged—Ha, here comes one who may help us," he went on. "Welcome back, Sir Giles. Have you any news?"

"Ay, your Majesty, lots," replied that capable knight, clanking up the hall. "But I have not found Golithos. His tower is empty except for miscellaneous rubbish, and the doors swing idly in the wind. He has flown." His voice was hoarse with weariness and his mail showed signs of hard travel.

"Flown, has he? And Mother Meldrum?"

"She also has flown—probably on a broomstick. Her house is dismantled and deserted, and doubtless the foul things of the haunted woods will hold their revels there to-night. Ugh!" He shuddered, for though he was dauntless where a reasonable number of caitiffs were concerned he had no taste for the supernatural.

"Strange," said the King musingly. "The plot thickens—But you are weary, Sir Giles. Pray seat yourself beside us while we consider the matter."

"Thanks, sire, but I prefer standing. I have sat some score of hours or more."

"I fear you will have to sit some more, good knight, for you must mount and lead your men again. Come, sirs, let us consider what course we are now to take."

CAPTIVES AGAIN

In a wood of scattered and stunted trees many miles from Banrive, Mother Meldrum was urging on her heavily loaded ass with the assistance of a cudgel. Beside her strode the gigantic form of Golithos, with a big bundle tied to his shoulders and carrying his mighty axe. There was a kind of horrible contentment about the two as they went along in silence only broken by an occasional chuckle from Golithos and the thumping of the cudgel as it came down on the animal's ribs. Round about them walked seven large black cats.

"We can take it a bit easier now," said Mother Meldrum at length. She had taken off her cloak and in her man's dress and with the false beard removed she looked a particularly hideous figure; the beard had at least hidden part of her face. "It's not far now to the barren rocks and nobody ever comes as near to them as this. Everything's going very nicely."

"Yes, isn't it," he said. "Do you know I got very worried, waiting outside the town with your bundles and the cats. I thought you'd never come. I was afraid something had happened and you couldn't find the little ones."

"That's because you're a fool," she said with her usual candour. "I got them almost at once, as I knew I would. Don't you start complaining about me!"

"No, of course not. But the cats worried me so much—snarling and rolling about and getting their ropes entangled. And when I tried to sort them out they simply bit pieces out of me. Look at my hands."

"Glad they did; I wish they'd done more to you. You lost one of my cats, too, you lout! If it doesn't come along soon, I'll remember it when we settle up."

"But it really wasn't my fault," he said quickly. "I just untied it a moment to disentangle it and it clawed me and bolted off. It'll come along all right."

"There'll be trouble for you if it doesn't. Now let's stop a bit and see how things are."

"Yes, let's," said Golithos eagerly.

"You keep away! No touching." She lifted up the lid of one of the baskets on the ass and untied the neck of a coarse sack within. "Aha, you're tired of grizzling now, are you? That's a good thing for you."

The head of Joe came out and stared at her, white and horrified.

"Get out and walk!" she ordered. "No, wait a bit: I'll have to tie your hands behind you."

She tied him up and lashed the rope to the huge bundle that formed the principal load of the ass. Then she went to the other basket and liberated Sylvia.

Poor Sylvia's eyes were swollen with weeping and her face showed a stunned horror. She shook with fear as she got out, her pretty silk dress with the golden flowers and bees all crumpled and stained with the filthy sack she had been tied in, and looked up in the old witch's face.

"Keep apart," she shouted, for Joe had got close to Sylvia to give her what consolation he could, which was not very much. "One on each side. Now march!"

They started off again, Joe and Sylvia walking in a dazed way on either side of her, Golithos coming behind with his load and leading the ass, and the cats surging about them like a pack of grim black hounds.

"You were clever to get them, the way you did." said Golithos, to put her in a good humour. "You seem to manage everything the way you want it."

"Oh, I'm clever enough. I just went in with my half-dozen fat hens and offered them for next to nothing, and I talked to the fat old cook about things in general until I saw these brats coming along and looking for something new. They got something new all right enough. I just gave them good morning and asked them if they knew of a nice quiet place in the garden where I could turn a little rabbit loose, because it was so cruel to keep a rabbit cooped up and it'd be much happier in the garden. And they took me to very nice quiet place, all thick bushes and the like. Ho, ho, ho! I had them twisted up in two sacks before they could begin to think what was happening. And by the time they'd started to yell I had them in the baskets and hopped on top of the ass and started the bagpipes. And some gardeners and people came running up and out but I went a-galloping and blowing the pipes and all they wanted was to see the last of me. And out in the street some stared at me and some pitched carrots and things at me, but I didn't stop blowing until I was clear out of Banrive. Ho, ho, ho!"

Golithos laughed hideously and the children cowered as they stumbled along. Mother Meldrum jerked furiously at the ropes that held them and told them to step out smartly if they didn't want some extra trouble.

"Don't make them walk too fast," said Golithos. "Poor things, it won't do to get them too tired! Children do get thin so easily," he added with a touch of pathos.

"They'll walk and you'll walk and I'll walk just as long as it suits me!" she shouted with one of her sudden changes to fury.

"Oh, yes, of course," he said hastily. "I was merely suggesting———"

"Well, don't. You've got your job to attend to before you need worry whether they're thin or fat. As soon as we get beyond the barren rocks you're finished with them until you've done your job."

"Oh, I'll do it all right," he said, twirling his gigantic axe. "The sight of them has done me ever so much good. I'll go back and just hide near Banrive until I get my chance. It won't take long because you tell me the King goes out hawking every other day or so and it won't be at all difficult to creep up when he's sitting on his fat old horse and staring up in the sky. I'll have him hacked to bits in no time. And if any twenty of his men come up I'll cut them all down, as I used to do in the fine old days." He roared with laughter and made the air whistle as he swung the axe over his head.

"At last I'm getting part of what I want," said Mother Meldrum as she watched him approvingly. "Only part, because there's others in the town I'm going to get square with. Wait till we're comfortably settled beyond the barren rocks and we'll be able to do quite a nice lot of damage one way and another. When they find their little children disappearing every now and then they'll wish they'd left me alone in my comfortable little town business and not got the King to turn me out."

Golithos did an ungainly dance of joy at the mention of a good supply of his natural food. "I suppose," he said when his transports had calmed down a little, "there's no chance of their finding the way through the rocks?"

"Not a bit of chance. The way through is by a hole just near the top of the big cliff, and even if they found the hole they'd lose their way in two minutes if they tried to follow the road. There's fifty little tunnels branching in all directions and I'm the only one who knows the right one. Besides, they wouldn't dare to follow us in: there's other things there besides bats and darkness. No, we'll be comfortable enough. There's an old tower which you can take for your very own, and there's a little house in the trees that will just suit me and I'll settle down very comfortably with my cats."

They trudged on in contented silence for a time. Sylvia and Joe were, luckily for them in one way, too stupefied with horror to realize the hideous fate that had come upon them and they went on as well as they could, Mother Meldrum occasionally hinting by a ferocious pick at the ropes that they were not walking fast enough.

THE BARREN ROCKS

Half an hour later Mother Meldrum gave a grunt of satisfaction. "Here we are at last," she said. "Look up, little dears, and see where you're going to climb to."

They had passed out of the thicker part of the stunted trees into an open space, and the shuddering children saw before them a deep ravine of dry and jagged rocks. On the farther side the walls rose in a cliff which, though not very much higher than they were standing, was very precipitous and evidently difficult to climb for anyone who did not know the path. Nowhere about the rocks was there any sign of life or vegetation. It was a new strange land on which a blight had fallen; a land over which a dull horror seemed to brood.

"We'll go down a nice little path I know of," said Mother Meldrum, with a deep chuckle, "and then we'll go up a nice little path I know of. And close to the top is a nice little tunnel I know of, and we'll go ever so far through it until we come to a nice little house I know of. Now don't you wish you hadn't run away from dear old Mother———"

She stopped and turned round and stared. Golithos, who had been grinning savagely at her words, stopped and looked quickly in the same direction.

"I thought I heard Gubbins," she said (Gubbins was the missing cat).

"Oh, I'm so glad!" he said, "I wouldn't have liked you to lose him. He must have caught us up. Ah, there he is! I thought he wouldn't be long in finding us."

"Yes, you fool!" snarled the old woman, choking with rage. "And see who's coming after him! This comes of trusting a lubber like you!"

"It's that Snerg again," said Golithos uneasily.

The children's hearts gave a bound of joy and hope. A long way off, and far beyond the black cat that came trotting up, they saw a little figure running. It was Gorbo, and the dead weight of terror seemed to lift from them at the sight.

"I don't seem able to shake him off somehow," went on Golithos, not at all with the air of a man who was ready to do great deeds. "But he hasn't seen us yet because we're hidden by these trees. Let's get into the thick part and hide until he comes up and then I'll jump out and cut him down before he can shout."

"Come along, you brats, or I'll murder you here!" shouted Mother Meldrum.

She dragged fiercely at the ropes and they had to follow her into the trees. Golithos hauled on the leading rope of the ass, and the ass, as its nature taught it to do, hauled back. With a howl of rage he took a firmer grip of the rope and dragged the ass a few feet. Then the rope snapped and the animal turned and trotted back on the path they had come.

"Now you've done it, you great lout!" screamed Mother Meldrum. "Now he'll know we're here! Oh, I'll settle accounts with you, Golithos, once we're out of this!"

"But there's no great harm done," pleaded Golithos. "He'll come along looking for us just the same. Oh, please keep quiet, he may be coming along now. If he hears us I won't be able to jump out on him!"

The old woman controlled herself sufficiently to keep silent, though her face was livid with rage. She dragged the children into a thicker part of the trees and pushed them over and crouched down by them, surrounded by her cats, who stopped still at an order from her and lay quiet on the ground. Golithos stooped behind a tree with his axe ready.

Gubbins, the missing cat, came trotting up. They could see him stop and sniff about. Then he looked back invitingly and saying "Me-reow! me-reow!" in a high and strong voice, came purring in among the trees and greeted his mistress and his brother cats. Mother Meldrum silenced him with a clump on the head and he too crouched down.

There was a dead silence for a minute or two. Then suddenly the witch gave a little grunt, for Gorbo came into view, walking with a silent tread and peering in all directions, with an arrow fitted to his bow.

HOW GORBO FOUND THE WAY

The measures taken by King Kul to search for the children would have, by themselves, resulted in failure and a tragedy. Though of an estimable character he was not remarkable for handling difficult situations, especially those which for want of a better term we must call matters of police. His dominion had been peaceable so long that he had lost the knack of it; besides, his subjects, an amiable but rather muddle-headed offshoot of mediæval, days, were of little assistance in the case, for no one could give information as to the road taken by the alleged old man with the ass and big baskets and bagpipes. The knights too—with the exception of Sir Giles, who had plenty of ginger in him (which is why he had secured the prettiest girl at court)—were rather lacking in practice owing to the decay of dragons, caitiffs, and other undesirable inhabitants, and they rather played at chivalrous doings than took any active interest in them. Consequently, though troops were sent searching in all directions, they went without definite instructions, and they merely wandered about, putting innocent people through severe cross-examinations, inspecting cock-lofts in lonely but peaceful farmhouses, and generally making themselves thoroughly disliked without obtaining any useful hints.

Sir Giles, however, had hit on an idea which had some reason at the back of it. The far western border of the land was some half-day's ride away and the country beyond, though no one knew anything definite about it, had a very unsavoury reputation. It was generally considered to be the part where the dragons and caitiffs and others had gone during the past few centuries, and he considered it probable that Mother Meldrum and Golithos had selected it as a suitable spot for their future home; therefore he had taken his squire and ten picked men and gone there at full speed. The idea, as I have said, was on the whole a good one. The one reason against its being a successful one was that Mother Meldrum and Golithos had gone in the opposite direction.

While King Kul was discussing the situation and making suggestions, King Merse rushed off with Gorbo and collected his men, and Vanderdecken joined them with his immediately afterwards. But they, like the others, had little notion of which would be the best direction to take until Gorbo gave them a second shock by making a really practical suggestion.

While the men were formed up and waiting for orders, with King Merse and Vanderdecken at their wits' end to know what orders to give, Gorbo suddenly ran off and peered between the legs of some citizens who formed a little crowd near the ancient Cloth Hall. The citizens were looking at a cat of exceeding bigness and blackness which was engaged with a bone. There were none present who had visited Mother Meldrum professionally so no one recognized this as one of her cats; they were merely wondering at its appearance, the cats of Banrive being as a rule small and either fawn colour or grey with stripes.

Gorbo acted with a promptness inspired by his grief and his knowledge that time was flying. He rushed to a fish stall and demanded a pound of sprats on the King's affairs and a straw-bag to put them in. He returned and, pushing his way through the crowd, offered the animal a sprat. It took it with a fierce growl and ate it, and then looked up hopefully for more. Gorbo did not give it another yet but patted and stroked it instead, allowing it to sniff at the bag.

"Did ums old cats want um sprats?" he said soothingly. "Then um good old cats must work for um sprats."

The animal, though evidently intelligent above its kind, could not of course wholly understand. It got easily as far as understanding that this small man (whom it remembered seeing before) was one who had control of fish in a bag, and he set up a roaring purr and rubbed hard against him in the hope that he would do the decent thing and give him another.

Gorbo held out another sprat and walked backwards towards his brother Snergs, the cat following.

"See!" he said to King Merse; "one of Mother Meldrum's cats! Perhaps it can lead us to her."

King Merse stared at him in wonder at his penetration. Vanderdecken smote Gorbo on the shoulder. "This man of yours is improving," he said. "We can but try it."

"We will," said the King. "Go ahead, Gorbo, with your cat, and we will follow some way behind."

The inhabitants were ordered to clear the road and Gorbo, after giving a third sprat for encouragement, walked towards the town gate. The cat followed him, chewing and growling. On arriving at a clear space beyond the walls Gorbo urged it by gestures to take the road. After a few moments it looked about and sniffed the ground; went on a bit and sniffed again. Gorbo looked on anxiously.

"Home to mother then!" he said, holding up his bag. "Home to other old black cats."

The animal turned and looked at him and then, giving a terrific wail, started off at a trot. Gorbo followed and the cat, merely stopping an instant to make sure that the bag of fish was coming close behind, went on down a narrow trail that led to some woods.

It went steadily on and Gorbo trotted steadily behind it. And a quarter of a mile or so behind them came the soft padding footsteps of the Snergs and the clumping of the Dutchmen's sea-boots as they followed at the double.

THE REFORM OF GOLITHOS

As Gorbo appeared in the open space beyond the trees, Mother Meldrum shook her fist fiercely at Golithos to encourage him, and for an instant had her attention taken away from the children. But this instant was enough for Joe, who had been working his hands loose from the rope (he had learned rope tricks in his circus life), and who now had them free. He quickly untied Sylvia's hands and then very gently helped her to her feet. "Run," he whispered close to her ear. And with a bound they were off, Joe holding her hand with a tight grip and hauling her along through the trees.

They heard a savage yell from behind them; but they were out in the open and running up to Gorbo, who sprang forward to meet them with a shout.

"Hide in the trees!" screamed Joe. "There's Golithos coming!"

Gorbo jumped and looked quickly round. Then in an instant he sprang with them into the shade of the trees on the other side of the open space. He gave a little sound of wonder and joy, something like a sob, and then faced round, again with his bow held ready. "Lie down and hide," he said, without turning his head

"But there's Golithos there!" wailed Sylvia. "Let's run, Gorbo!"

"Not me," said Gorbo. "Just lie quiet."

There was a dead silence for a time. Then they heard the voice of Golithos hailing from the opposite side of the open spot.

"Is that you, Gorbo?" he called.

"It's me," replied Gorbo.

"Look here," went on the voice, "you go away and I'll let you keep the little ones. There!"

"Thanks," said Gorbo.

"Oh, but do be reasonable. Let's talk it over quietly; it's no good being unfriendly. Just come out in the open and we'll talk it over."

"All right," said Gorbo. "You come too." He walked to the edge of the trees and stood looking across at the other side.

"But I can't see you," said Golithos. "You must really show some confidence in me, and then I'll come."

"Will this suit you?" Gorbo walked out some half-dozen steps.

"Yes, that's better, Gorbo. You see I don't want to harm you." (From their hiding-place the children could hear him blundering through the bushes and twigs.) "I've always rather liked you and if we can just talk over matters———"

With a rush and roar he sprang out, his mighty axe swung up high.

Whang.

Golithos stopped his rush within six feet of Gorbo and stood swaying. His axe fell crashing to the ground.

Whang—Whang.

Golithos toppled and fell headlong with a thump that shook the ground. Three arrows stuck out from behind his head.

MOTHER MELDRUM GOES

The children flung themselves at Gorbo and hugged him, and Sylvia was shaking with sobs. He squeezed them to him for just one instant and then jumped away. "Where's Mother Meldrum?" he said quickly.

"She's in there," replied Joe, pointing across.

Gorbo crept up cautiously, looking about him as he went. Suddenly he gave an exclamation. "Look!" he cried, pointing to the opposite side of the ravine.

The old witch was climbing, climbing up the rocks, and behind her came the black cats. Gorbo rushed to the edge of the ravine and shot. The arrow fell short. He shot again and again, but it was useless; the distance was too great for a bow. And Mother Meldrum climbed and climbed, with an agility and strength that appeared miraculous.

Gorbo turned again, for there was a mighty trampling behind him. Up came the Snergs and the Dutch seamen, headed by their leaders. The children and fallen body of Golithos took but an instant of their attention for Gorbo shouted that Mother Meldrum was escaping.

The Snergs ranged along the edge of the ravine and shot thick and fast so that the air was full of arrows, but the old witch was well out of range and she knew it. She had reached a flat part near the summit of the cliff, and the tunnel that led through the barren rocks was close at hand. With a shrill screaming laugh that sounded horridly across the ravine she danced a fantastic dance of triumph, something between an Irish jig and a coranto. O hideous sight!

But little did this hag of mediæval days know of the strides of science. The voice of Vanderdecken (who had so wisely trained his seamen in the part) rang out:

"Musketeers, advance! Handle your muskets! Cock your muskets! Aim your muskets! Fire! Recover your muskets!"

At the word "Fire," three-and-thirty shots shook the air and echoed from the rocky crags. A dark cloud of smoke hung over the scene.

The smoke drifted away.

"Where," said King Merse, "is Mother Meldrum?"

Vanderdecken handed him his telescope. "There is something like bits of rags sticking on the rocks," he said. "And I think I can see a hand hanging over the edge of the cliff. See what you can make of it."

"Yes," agreed King Merse as he looked, "it is undoubtedly as you say. That is Mother Meldrum—or part of her"

Thus it was. When three-and-thirty muskets of the kind made in Vanderdecken's day, loaded with double bullets and a half handful of buckshot, are fired simultaneously by expert marksmen at the same target the result is effective. Mother Meldrum had been blown to bits.

ALL TROUBLES OVER

There was a good deal of ringing of bells at Banrive when the joyous band of Snergs and Dutchmen arrived with the children safe and sound, and it was known that Golithos and Mother Meldrum had passed away.

The ass had been found trying to rub its load off against a tree, and the Snergs had untied the bundles and selected whatever there was of value in them and thrown the rest away. Then they put Joe and Sylvia on the ass and started back, singing sea chanties which the Dutchmen had taught them. Sylvia soon got over the worst of her shock, and though she was a good deal worried about the crumpled and dirty state of her pretty new dress, she was able in time to join modestly in the chorus. Joe did not have so much shock to get over because he was the sort that does not trouble about troubles that are past and he sang lustily.

Gorbo was given the place of honour in front and he came along with a light step although he was carrying Golithos' enormous axe, which was his according to the rules of war. He was the subject of a good deal of jovial badinage on account of the cat Gubbins, which had not gone to join its brother cats (now doubtless great hunters in the land of barren rocks) but had attached itself to him. It may have been that it liked Gorbo's cast of countenance or it may have been that it considered a man with a bag of fish something to stay by, but I leave this for naturalists to decide; all I know is that it went ahead of him, with its tail well up, stepping rather in the manner of goats belonging to certain British regiments.

King Kul embraced the children, almost with tears, and with his own hands gave Sylvia the puppy, which had been wandering disconsolately about looking for them. He made a speech thanking the Snergs and the seamen for their great service in his dominions. When King Merse told him that Gorbo had slain Golithos single-handed he merely said, "Indeed? And very creditable of him—considering." He could never quite overcome his dislike of Gorbo.

But nobler feelings prevailed. He went to his privy-chambers and rummaged in a little chest of drawers. Returning to the hall he bade Gorbo approach and kneel.

"By this," he said, placing round his neck a cherry-coloured ribbon with a medallion, "I make you a Companion of the Order of Errant Tinkers. See that you wear it worthily."

Amid a murmur of applause the blushing Gorbo rose and thanked him gratefully and retired backwards. He was filled with a pride and joy that left him dizzy. At last it was officially recognized that he had escaped from the reproach of being the biggest fool of the race of Snergs. Sylvia and Joe ran to him and demanded to see. The medallion was a tasteful thing, representing a man in full armour mending a saucepan (Sir Bors, a tinker knighted on the field of battle). The order was an ancient one and Gorbo had full reason to be proud. It carried with it the freedom of the City and the right to remove his boots (if they hurt him) in the presence of the King.

The Lady Ermyntrude took charge of the children and told them to change into their Watkyns Bay uniforms (which had been washed and ironed) while their new clothes were sent to the dry cleaners. These were expeditious people and they promised to have them restored to their original beauty by noon on the following day; to the great joy of Sylvia, who loved her dress with the golden bees.

It was a happy time for all. Sir Giles returned in a very peevish frame of mind at the ill-success of his journey, but when he heard that the children had been brought safely back he came clashing in and embraced them with ardour. He said that perchance now they would let him look forward to a good night's rest. He changed from his travel-stained armour into a suit of murrey-coloured velvet in which he looked rather well, and he sat with the Lady Ermyntrude behind some curtains and held her hand, in spite of her warnings that people would see. Baldry (who I fear will never learn) tried to promote the gaiety of courts by creeping behind him and smiting him on the head with his bladder-stick; but he had to flee from the palace and hide for the rest of the day, since the King refused to grant him protection, saying: "Now perhaps you'll think before acting."

BACK ACROSS THE RIVER

Another day passed and then, at an early hour, the homeward journey was begun. Cheerful farewells were exchanged and amid the shouts of the populace the Expeditionary Force passed out of the town-gate which they had entered with such doubtful anticipations a few days before, with Joe and Sylvia riding on small ponies (wearing their fancy clothes) and two sumpter-mules in the charge of responsible churls. One mule was laden with presents from King Kul for the royal house of Snerg and other presents for Miss Watkyns and her staff (including some curiously wrought silver cups and an antique carved unicorn's horn suitable for a centre-piece), and the second mule bore two barrels of special wine for Vanderdecken.

King Kul promised to visit the Snergs if something in the way of a bridge could be made across the deep river, and Vanderdecken said he would give thought to the matter and devise a substantial swinging bridge that would not wobble too much.

They stayed for the night at the comfortable little castle of the Lord of the King's Marches, who was at home when they arrived and who, they found, was an agreeable man though with a slight touch of pomposity, like his steward. He accepted apologies for their former invasion of his stronghold and occupation of his best beds, and was quite nice about it, telling them that he appreciated the urgency of the case and they were heartily welcome. He seemed on the whole rather relieved to find his job gone. Throughout a long life he had been (nominally) guarding the border against a chance attack of Snergs, and now they had proved to be a good-natured and friendly people and he might have just as well been attending to other matters. He said that in future he would devote his time to gardening, for which he had a passion.

They bade him farewell in the morning and in a few hours were on the precipitous cliff that overhung the river, where they were greeted with great joy by the band of Snergs who had been left there to prevent any interference with the rope. They had made a little fort with a trench round it and they had sentries posted in the proper way. King Merse gave them a word or two of soldierly praise.

Sylvia was sent across with Tiger in a large basket, which the seamen rigged up in the manner of life-saving devices, and arrived safely, though rather giddy and frightened owing to the terrific height over which she had passed. Joe declined to go in the basket and jerked himself across the rope at great speed, as did the Snergs and Dutchmen. The presents were then put in the basket and hauled across, and then came the two barrels of wine. Vanderdecken superintended the lashing up of these himself as he said he wasn't going to take any silly risks with them. Gorbo swarmed over (amid cheers and laughter) with the cat clinging to his person, because they could not induce it to go in the basket.

BACK TO THE TOWN

It was only a league or a bit more to the town, where the news had already arrived. As the children drew near they noticed three figures conspicuous for their height among the small Snergs. Miss Watkyns, together with the Misses Scadging and Gribblestone, had come on good steady bears on the previous day to meet them, and there they had heard for the first time of their terrible final adventure.

When they saw the children coming along in their beautiful costumes of a long bygone age, they burst into weeping. This, though something in accord with the character of two of these ladies, came rather as a surprise from Miss Watkyns, who loathed display of sentiment. But she did not weep much. With a stern word to the others to have done with sloppiness she asked both children whether they were, or were not, thoroughly ashamed of themselves. It occurred to both Sylvia and Joe at this point that perhaps they ought to be, and they said they were ashamed. I believe this to be true, though most of the feeling wore off in ten minutes.

It is almost unnecessary to say that this was the occasion for a feast, and it must be noted that Gorbo no longer sat in the suburbs but was only seven places down from the King. In addition to the Order of Errant Tinkers (regarded rather enviously by many present) a brazen nutmeg glittered upon his breast, for King Merse felt that he had fairly earned it.

BACK TO WATKYNS BAY

IT occurs to me here that there is some difficulty in proving a really useful moral from this tale, although I have almost boastfully referred to it as coming in due course for the instruction of my younger readers. For however reprehensible the children were in their disobedience and irresponsibility it cannot be denied that the general results of their conduct were beneficial. They were instrumental in bringing a swift finish to two persons who constituted a serious menace to the public. They had brought about the establishment of friendly relations between two countries, and removed doubts that had existed for centuries. Lastly, they had returned magnificently dressed and bearing expensive gifts. So perhaps the only definite moral that can be deduced is, if you by any chance meet an ogre who claims to be reformed, pretend to believe him until you have got a gun and then blow his head off at the first opportunity.

On their arrival at Watkyns Bay the other children crowded round Sylvia and Joe with cries of delight and admiration, for nothing more gorgeous had been seen even in a picture-book, and there was at this point some danger of the swollen-headedness which Miss Watkyns had dreaded. But she soon put it right by ordering them both to change into their plain but serviceable two-piece garments, and stating that the others should be kept for very special occasions, such as fancy-dress affairs. This, by the way, led to the institution of fancy-dress dances and caused a great deal of extra needlework and ironing.

Sylvia and Joe were very glad to get back to their little cots with the hop mattresses, and when at last they dropped off to sleep (very late, for there was a good deal of whispering because the other children wanted to hear more) lulled by the distant breaking of the sea and the light rubbing of cinnamon bears against the fence without, they felt very peaceful and happy and resolved to be really good for a reasonably long time.

TO FINISH UP

Vanderdecken set to work and made a neat swinging bridge, light but strong, across the deep river, and King Kul made a visit to the Snergs and spent two days at Watkyns Bay. He distributed the prizes at the term end, and made one of those speeches about even little children having their responsibilities. Invitations had been sent to Joe and Sylvia and six other children to attend the wedding of Sir Giles and Lady Ermyntrude, but Miss Watkyns thanked His Majesty deeply and said she thought it inadvisable for them to go, as tending to unsettle their minds. She sent a wedding-present of a dainty tortoise-shell toilet and manicure-set, and the bride wrote to her on a piece of parchment that she considered it the most charming of all her presents. It was really good; it had been bought in Bond Street, at an expensive shop. Baldry overdid it at last at the wedding and got seven days. He had buttered the steps of the palace hall.

Gorbo is passing the time quite nicely, occasionally doing a job of work but more often resting. Gubbins, the black cat, sticks close to him and travels with him everywhere. It has great ability for catching game, such as birds and young rabbits and the like, and has learned to retrieve quite well, so Gorbo has his hunting cat like the Egyptian kings of old. He goes now and then to visit at Banrive and see what new trouble Baldry has got into, and to pay his respects to the King. He never fails to say, "Oh, this corn of mine!" and pulls off one boot.

The door in the region of twisted trees and the one on the other wide were built up with masonry. It was agreed that though Gorbo and the children found enormous supplies of mushrooms in the cavern, there was a nasty flavour of magic about the place and it was as well to leave it alone. I never heard what happened in the dark woods after Mother Meldrum had gone and the bats and other grisly things had it all to themselves, because no one, I believe, ever went there, which shows sense.

The knight Sir Percival gave up chivalrous doings on the day that he had the adventure at the castle. He did not slacken his anxious pace until he was back at his own little moated grange, and there he hung his armour and lance over the fireplace in the hall and decided to live quietly, and if he could not get a wife except by fighting for her, to go without. He went in for breeding a superior kind of pig and did rather well at it, taking several prizes.

Vanderdecken and his men make special efforts every now and then to clean up the old ship for her voyage home; but there is so much to do, what with weeds and barnacles and the gear having to be rove afresh and so forth, that they generally get tired of it after a short spell and say to the effect that it is no good overworking and it would be best to go for a day or two's hunting with the Snergs. It is my belief that they never will go away. And there is no particular reason why they should; things are very well as they are.

There is little more to tell now. It is possible that Joe and Sylvia may be sent to England if suitable new parents can be found for them, this being the usual thing after some years with the Society (but not of course years in the ordinary way), but I don't know if anything definite has been done in the matter. It is my opinion that Miss Watkyns will not let them go for a long time because they certainly keep the place lively. She tried to make them have a sense of responsibility by giving them charge of a new arrival, a little girl who was very thin and weepy, but the result was she became a riotous handful and broke a window for fun.

Tiger is doing well, though he had a touch of distemper last August. But nothing serious.

Lack of space prevents me from going into details of costs, etc., of the S.R.S.C., which is to be regretted as I am sure they would prove of absorbing interest to my more serious readers. I will therefore merely state that the Society is flourishing and on a sound financial basis, and that Miss Watkyns and the other ladies have an immense amount of work to do, which keeps them fit, sundry improvements of buildings and extensions having been put in hand at Watkyns Bay. The children go on happily year after year, slowly increasing in numbers as fresh cases arrive, and they splash about in the sea and play their various games and roam the woods and fleet the time carelessly as they did in the golden world.

The End

Printed in Great Britain
by Amazon